RBrauner ♡

FALLING IN LOVE

a moment

TOO LATE

CAN HAPPEN IN THE BLINK OF AN EYE

For Crystal.
For your unwavering support and friendship.
For your love of books and ability to fall in love with the stories we create.

a moment
TOO LATE

Falling in love can happen in the blink of an eye.

I fell for Jay the moment I laid eyes on him. Was drawn to
him in a way I'd never been drawn to a man before.
He was everything I wanted.
The man I dreamed about at night and looked for
everywhere I turned just for a glimpse of his perfection.
But I couldn't have him.
It was against the rules. Forbidden.
He was my best friend's boyfriend.
I would never do that to her.
Then she died.
Looking at him became painful, bringing back memories
of the reason we couldn't be together.
The reason I never pursued him.
I had to move on and vowed never to look back in an
attempt to escape him and the devastation in my heart.
Yet here I stand, five years later, staring into the eyes of the
man I still want. In the place I swore I'd never return to.
With memories assaulting me from every angle.
He's still the picture of perfection in my eyes, making our
attraction even more dangerous than it once was.
The only difference...
No one is standing in our way this time.

FALLING IN LOVE

a moment
TOO LATE

CAN HAPPEN IN THE BLINK OF AN EYE

prologue

My phone has vibrated in the pocket of my dress no less than ten times since class started thirty minutes ago. If I were in a lecture hall with five hundred other people, I'd risk checking to see who was calling at this early hour, but this professor is an asshole. The sight of my phone will set him off. On the first day of class, he made his stance on phones perfectly clear.

If he sees one, we all suffer.

In our second class, we found out exactly what suffering meant when someone walked in texting. The class hadn't even started. We weren't on his time yet. Still, he issued a ten-page paper and only gave us three days to do it.

Not a single person has been seen on their phone since.

Message received. Loud and clear.

My phone starts up again, and instantly the hairs on the back of my neck stand up, a chill running down my spine. Whoever keeps calling, it must be important which worries me. All my friends know all about this professor. I've complained about him on more than one occasion, so they know never to call during class.

Not to mention they're probably sound asleep. I'm the only idiot who signed up for classes that start before noon in my final semester of college. I didn't have much of a choice. This class is required to graduate, and this was the only time it was offered.

Sighing, I brush off my concerns and attempt to concentrate on the lecture my professor is droning on about. I'm barely able to keep my eyes open as I listen to his monotone voice go on and on about our final project, due in less than four weeks. I didn't get back in town until after ten last night, then I overslept, having to forgo stopping for coffee on the way to class so I wasn't late. Another one of the professor's pet peeves.

Graduation is just around the corner, though. No more early classes. No more asshole professors. Four years of hard work and dedication all come down to the next few weeks.

This semester has been mentally challenging. Both on a personal and professional level if you count being a college student by day and waitress by night a profession.

My days are long, the nights even longer. The much-needed rest and relaxation I was hoping for while vacationing last week never happened. Sleep eluded me most of spring break. I should have been sunbathing and sipping fruity drinks with little umbrellas in them. I was in paradise with no responsibilities. My days were my own, but they were lonely.

That's not a new concept it seems. I could be in a room surrounded by all my favorite people and I'd still feel lonely these days.

I spent the first day crying my eyes out behind large, black sunglasses while my parents went on a day excursion. It was beautiful outside, the water was clear, the light breeze keeping me from overheating. The view was breathtaking. I should have been enjoying it with a smile on my face. Or at the very least, taking a nap and working on my tan.

What did I do instead?

Once I knew my parents were gone, I went back to my room and curled up under the covers. My eyes were puffy and red. It hurt to keep them open. I was exhausted from my early flight, but aside from being physically tired, I was emotionally drained.

My heart was splintering in my chest. Every time I thought about that night, I felt a new fault line appear. It wouldn't be long before it shattered and there would be nothing left.

Because I gave him my heart two years ago.

Willingly.

Without asking for anything in return.

I expected him to treat it with care. To guard it. To keep it safe.

What did he do with it? Nothing.

That was only my first mistake, though. My second?

I didn't ask if he wanted it. Nope. I ripped it from my chest, shoved it in his hands, and smiled. It happened so fast I didn't give it a second thought. There was no time to overthink what I was doing because it was over before I knew it even happened.

Why was I so reckless? Because there was something there. The moment I saw him I felt it, the connection. It was magnetic, the pull I felt toward him. The way he held me in his arms was heavenly, as if I was meant to be held by him and only him.

Love at first sight.

I was crazy, right? That never happens in real life. Sure, you read about it in romance novels, but I've never heard about it happening to anyone I know. Hell, my mother said it took her two years to get my dad to open his eyes. He says he was just waiting to see if she was worth the effort.

Great role models, right?

But after twenty-five years of marriage, two petitions for divorce that were eventually withdrawn, and one affair on my father's part, they seem to be doing okay.

That's a lie.

My parents tolerate each other at best. Neither of them are getting any younger, and I think they're afraid of dying alone. My father turns sixty-one this year, and my mother will be sixty. At that age, who wants to start over?

I'd be scared, too.

Hell, I'm scared right now.

Of the way I feel for him. Of the power he has over me. The power to destroy my heart. Power I gave him without a second though.

You're an idiot, Andrea.

Yup. Even my subconscious knows what a big mistake I made.

Four more weeks. Then I can leave here and start over. I'll take what's left of my heart and pray there's someone out there who can mend the broken pieces. Someone who's meant just for me.

Shaking away the thoughts, I turn my attention back to my professor. He's walking my way, his eyes locked on mine. Either I've been busted for zoning out or he's just having a bad day. The scowl on his face gives nothing away. It's the same expression he's worn since day one.

"You have ten minutes to decide your topic. Please turn them in to Ms. Morris." He motions to me, and I wave enthusiastically. It's more for show than anything. Maybe if I smile and pretend to be excited he'll think I was paying attention after all. "She'll bring them to my office after class."

Or not.

He's definitely aware I zoned out. This is my punishment. I get to run across campus to drop off topics to him and sprint back in less than fifteen minutes for my next class. It won't be easy, especially considering I chose to wear a dress and heeled sandals today, but I'll make it work.

At least my next professor isn't a dick. He probably won't even notice if I slip in late.

Taking the large, manila envelope he's extended in my direction, I nod in understanding and avert my eyes quickly. I still have to come up with my own topic, and I've spent the last forty minutes mentally beating myself up.

Didn't I just do that for the last seven days?

Sure did, and it ruined what should have been a perfect vacation in paradise. It's about time I stop.

That's the thing about guilt. It refuses to let go of the grip it has on your soul. It wraps itself around you and holds on for the ride, laughing the entire time.

Look at the wrong person, guilt smacks you across the face.

Think about them, guilt's there to remind you why you shouldn't.

Get close enough to smell their woodsy scent? Throat punch.

Guilt is a bitch. The only way to get rid of it is to clear your conscience.

Like you have the balls to do that.

She's right. I don't. Because telling my truth would destroy more lives than my own. And if I'm going to hell, I don't find it necessary to bring company.

Four more weeks.

I can survive that long. I'll just lock myself in my apartment. I've been doing it all semester, what's a few more weeks? Everything is going to be fine.

I'll suffer so she doesn't have to.

I'll pretend I'm not miserable, that my heart's not broken, the way I have been the last two years.

My heart for hers.

By keeping what happened a secret, I'm saving her from the heartbreak. That's what friends do. They jump in front of a moving car to push you out of the way. They sacrifice themselves, their own happiness, so you can find yours.

As soon as the professor is out the door, students crowd my desk, thrusting papers in my face. I slide them all in the envelope one by one and stare down at my blank form. I'm the last one left. Alone.

Again.

You would think I'd be used to the silence by now. I live alone. Spend my nights locked in my apartment. I've pushed my friends away and barely answer my phone.

I'm the reason I'm isolated.

I'm the one responsible for feeling lonely.

I've done this to myself and I have no one else to blame.

Well, I could start pointing fingers, but at this point, why bother? It won't change what happened two years ago or three months ago. No one can erase the past. We either learn from it, try to be better, overcome the obstacles, and grow as a person. Or we wallow, allowing ourselves to suffer in silence.

It feels like I'm constantly teetering somewhere in the middle. I'd love to say I've learned my lesson, but I find myself wallowing more often than not.

Attempting to focus, I'm feverishly scribbling when

another chill washes over me, this one more pronounced than the last. Goosebumps pebble my exposed legs, a shiver making it's way up my spine. I'm rubbing them with my free hand when I hear the soft click of the door, followed by the vibration of my phone again.

Finally removing it from the confines of my pocket, I find Summer's face smiling at me. My second mom. The one who adopted me into her family the first day I met her. Who's shown me more love in the two years I've known her than my parents have in my twenty-two years of life.

Sliding my finger across the screen to answer, I greet her warmly, a huge smile on my face. I missed seeing her this morning at the Java Bean. Not only did I need the caffeine, but her hugs make everything better. Not feeling well? Get a hug from Summer. Fail an exam? Summer's hug will make you forget about it.

There is no limit to the power of her hugs. Summer's heart is so big you can feel her love when she hugs you.

The way she says my name has alarm bells sounding in my head. I can almost hear the tears streaming down her cheeks, her big, beautiful heart breaking in her chest.

And when she finally tells me why she's calling, I feel the remnants of my already fragile heart shatter. Her words bring tears to my eyes, clouding my vision, my smile fading as the phone falls from my hands. The screen cracks as it hits the floor, but I barely register the sound.

Suddenly I'm being pulled out of my chair, my legs wobbling slightly, and into his warm embrace. He's fresh from a shower, the woodsy scent enveloping me, causing my heart to studder.

Home.

That's what it feels like to be wrapped in his arms. But right now, not even he can calm the frantic beat of my heart as it pounds against my rib cage. The *thump, thump, thump* rattling in my ears is the only indication I'm not dreaming.

This can't be happening.

"I've got you," he whispers as his hand runs up and down my back.

My fists are tightly gripping the front of his soft T-shirt. I can feel the rapid beating of his heart beneath my hands, whereas mine suddenly feels like it's come to a complete stop.

When my legs give out, he scoops me up and sits with me in his lap. I can't even bring myself to fight him. Tension and guilt are swirling around me, taunting me, but it's no match for the devastation that's pressing on my chest.

"Breathe, Drea," I hear him say as he tucks a piece of stray hair behind my ear. "Just breathe."

In. Out. In. Out.

Easy, right? Yet I can't seem to catch my breath. I've never been able to with him this close.

"I have to go," I say, scrambling off his lap, gathering all my things and shoving them in my messenger bag. I'm out the door, his protests cut off when it closes behind me.

Four weeks. I can survive four more weeks. Then I'm gone. I'll leave this place behind me and never look back.

There's nothing left here for me now anyway.

one

FIVE YEARS. NOT LONG ENOUGH.

Which becomes evident the moment I see the number flashing across my screen. The area code alone brings back memories of those last few months. With the anniversary less than a week away, seeing his name and smiling face cause my stomach to churn and my heart to ache.

I left that part of my life behind me and never looked back. It was too painful ... even now. Not just to remember what happened but to see the people I called friends back then. They're all a reminder of what we lost. Of the events that changed our lives forever.

It's amazing how one night can alter your entire future.

I should answer but I'm frozen, my finger poised to slide across the screen; my fear paralyzing me the way it always does when I think about my past.

If I answer, I'll hear his voice. The nightmares of that day and the weeks following will become fresh in my mind again. Everything will be as real as it was then, and I'm not sure I can handle reliving the moment my heart broke.

If I'm being honest with myself, I never really dealt with it to begin with. I ran away. As soon as I had the chance. Without saying good-bye. Then, as the city limit sign became smaller and smaller in my rear-view mirror, I vowed I'd never look back. I knew I was being a coward and I accepted that. After all the tears I shed, I couldn't bear to look into their eyes even one last time.

The ringing stops, my screen fading to black after a few seconds, yet I can still see his face. I haven't released the breath I sucked in thirty seconds ago as shock radiated through my body. My lungs are starting to burn but I can't seem to let go. Maybe it's because I know this isn't over yet. He's never been one to give up easily.

Hell, I'm not sure he's ever given up on anything since I met him. Strong willed is putting it nicely. Stubborn is a more accurate description. Pain in my ass was always my favorite term.

All reasons I loved him.

My hope is that he's changed. Maybe this will be the one time he lets it go, whatever it is, the reason he's calling.

Who am I kidding? I know exactly why he's calling. I've been expecting this call for years, yet it hasn't come until now.

Year one I held my phone in my hand all day expecting it to ring. Or a text message to appear. Something, anything from my past to rear it's ugly head. Because the heartache didn't fail to consume me that day, nor did the buckets of tears I cried.

Year two, I left my phone was on vibrate in my pocket just in case. I didn't want to hear from them. To talk about what happened. I was convinced the first year was a fluke, that they were going to call, but they never did.

The last two years, I kept my phone close to me but something inside of me told me it wasn't going to ring. After years of silence, there was no reason to reach out at that point. It was just another day, even though my heart didn't get the memo.

I should have known it would ring this year. Should have prepared for this moment. Red wine and ice cream are not going to get me through the rest of the night if I'm forced to answer this call.

When my phone doesn't begin ringing again, I close my eyes and slowly exhale. Maybe he really isn't going to push the issue. It would be a first, but stranger things have happened.

The pain in my chest is barely beginning to subside when I hear my phone beep, my eyes flying back open as I suck in a new breath.

Nope. Not giving up.

SPENCER: Avoiding me? That's not very nice, Andi. I used to be your favorite. We used to be friends.

Past tense. I wonder if he even realizes what he's said.

My fingers are poised to type a response when my phone starts ringing in my hand. There's no avoiding him or his call. He's going to continue pestering me until I answer him. Mainly because he knows I'll give in eventually.

Spence would poke and poke and poke until we all gave in and he got his way. Whatever he wanted, he didn't stop until he had it—from picking where we ordered takeout to what movie we were going to watch. If he had his heart set on something, he refused to give up.

Which means I will have to answer the phone.

Text feels like the safer route, and if I were at work, I'd have a believable excuse as to why I can't take his call. Being that it's Sunday, he'll know I'm lying, and I've never been a good liar. I wear my emotions on my sleeve like a badge of honor.

"Hello, Spencer," I state, attempting to keep my voice from shaking as I greet him with feigned enthusiasm.

"Andi. It's been a long time." He always was one to point out the obvious. "I'm surprised you gave in so easily. The Andi I knew would have made me try a little harder to get her on the phone. I had my money on at least three texts and five calls. Mia even guessed it would take at least two of each."

The mention of Mia has me running my fingers through my hair and checking for split ends. I'd like to think she would be proud of me. For as much as I mess with my hair—straightening and curling it on a daily basis —it's still healthy and free of damaging boxed hair dye. The worst product on the planet according to Mia. She would cringe whenever we walked down the aisle at the grocery store and passed the dozens upon dozens of tiny boxes.

"How much money did I cost you?" I ask, releasing my hair and letting the long curl fall across my chest.

Without Mia to style my hair, I haven't cut more than necessary off in the last five years. A trim here and there to keep it healthy. I used to wear it just below my shoulders, framed around my face by long bangs. Those bangs have since grown out and it's past the middle of my back.

"Nothing this time. We were both wrong, so no money is going to exchange hands."

My hand flies to my mouth, covering the laugh that threatens to burst from my chest. Spence should know better. He may think he gets to keep his money but I'm sure Mia already has a plan for it and is currently on her Target or Amazon app making a purchase he won't find out about until weeks after it's arrived.

"Not to cut to the chase, but why are you calling, Spencer?" I ask, shaking away a memory of Mia with a sinister smirk on her face, palm out for Spencer to hand over his credit card the last time he lost a bet to her.

"Don't you miss me?"

That's a loaded question because I do. I miss all the friends I made in Great Falls, but the real answer is no. I can't miss him. Because missing him, missing any of them, is too painful. And Spencer and Mia stayed after I ran.

"Spencer," I growl, avoiding answering him.

"Listen, there is a reason for the call, but before I tell you I have a favor to ask."

"Of course you do. You can ask, but I won't make you a promise I can't keep. You know that." My voice is strong even though my hands are starting to shake.

When Spencer asks you for a favor, you proceed with caution. I fell for his innocent smile the first time and learned the hard way not to trust it. I'm sure he's sporting the same smile right now, even though I can't see him.

"Just keep an open mind before I tell you why I'm calling." Or maybe he's not smiling considering the serious tone he's taking with me. When I don't respond, he continues anyway, "Next Saturday is—"

"I know what it is, Spencer. Kind of hard to forget."

As much as I've tried to ignore the looming date, it's one that never goes unnoticed. It's almost as if the calendar turns to March and the countdown begins. Ten days, then five. The days slowly tick by, taunting me with a constant reminder of what's coming. Of what happened. Of the day I lost a piece of myself. The day my life was forever altered.

The reason I ran away from everyone I ever loved.

"Yeah. Trust me, I know. I'm still here. I relive that day more than most. But this year is the five-year anniversary, and the university and the town are putting together a remembrance, a celebration of life. Summer said she tried to contact you, but you never called her back."

Summer's called at least six times in the last week alone. Every single time I see her name on my screen I'm brought to tears. Not just one here or there, either. I full on broke down sobbing in my car for almost fifteen minutes the other day. My makeup was destroyed. My eyes were still red and puffy when I got home from work hours later. There's no way I'd be able to survive hearing the sorrow in her voice, let alone the blame in her stare. I couldn't even bring myself to say good-bye to her when I left.

"I've been meaning to," I lie.

"I'm going to let that slide for now." There's a long pause before Spencer asks me the one question I have been dreading since my phone started ringing. There's only one reason he was calling. The one reason I was scared to answer the phone. Afraid I wouldn't be able to deny him his request. "Will you come back for the ceremony?"

"I can't." The words slip past my lips before I give them a second thought.

"You're going to have to do better than that. I dare you to come up with a damn good reason you won't be here to remember your best friend. To remember the person she was and the life that was cut short. You're not the only one who's still grieving, Andrea. None of us have closure, and sometimes it feels like the wound is as fresh as it was that morning. I'm hoping next weekend will help me move on. Help all of us close the door on that chapter of our lives and move forward.

"I won't lie to you and tell you that it's going to be easy. Hell, it's probably going to be harder than I'm expecting it to be. If all of us are here, together, maybe that will help.

And you're the last one to agree. The only person holding out. The stubborn one of the group."

"I'm pretty sure that's you," I counter when he takes a breath, clearly frustrated with the fact I'm not giving in to his request. I can't. I won't be able to handle it. If I break down every year from two thousand miles away, it's only going to be intensified if I'm back there. Where it happened. In the place that has the power to destroy me all over again.

It doesn't matter if I'll be surrounded by people who love me. Who've gone through the same thing. Loss is a crushing feeling, and my heart almost didn't survive the first time. It hasn't healed from the original blow.

"When it comes to the people I love, maybe I am a little hardheaded. It's because I care. And honestly, I don't want to do this without you. It wouldn't feel right."

Vivid images of Sam laughing, singing at karaoke night, purposely spilling drinks on rude customers with a sinister smirk on her face fills my mind. She was a wild child with a heart of gold. Her personality radiated off her in waves. From her funky hair to her second-hand clothes. Her style was her own—unique and quirky—and she was proud of it.

She didn't want to be like everyone else. She did everything she could to stand out. It wasn't for the attention, like most people assumed until they got to know her. No, Sam was afraid to blend in with the rest of the town. She was a big city girl living in a small town.

I miss her.

Every day.

Every time I pass a coffee shop I think of her. She always smelled like freshly roasted coffee beans. Her nails more often than not had coffee grounds under them. And even when she wasn't working, she had a coffee in her hand.

It's why I've taken to drinking store-bought iced coffee. I haven't visited a coffee shop or made a freshly brewed cup of coffee in years. I don't even own a coffee maker anymore. The only coffee I consume is premade, flavored, crappy bottled coffee I buy in bulk. Vanilla and caramel, never mocha. Mocha was my favorite.

"Fine," I hear myself mumble. What did I just agree to? *Torture, plain and simple.* "I'll be there, just tell me when and where."

"I'll make you a reservation at the Hideaway and email you the information." His voice remains flat, void of all emotion. I was expecting him to be elated with the fact I agreed so easily, but it seems my decision has made this all real for him. "And, Andi, thank you. It'll be nice to see you, even if the circumstances bring back some of the most painful memories."

Painful? Sure, but I'd go with a stronger word. Agonizing. Excruciating.

Take your pick on how to describe the feeling that's been shackled around my heart for the last five years. I still can't find an adjective to accurately define it.

My best friend was murdered.

Because of me.

I don't think there are any words in the dictionary that can accurately define how I feel every morning when I wake up.

Shame for the secrets I kept from her.

Regret for my actions that led up to that night.

Guilty I'm still alive and she's gone.

I've made a habit of washing away all those feeling in the shower each and every morning. I try not to carry the weight of Sam's death with me to work. I can't let the burden I feel get in the way of my job. I need to have a clear head at all times, and thinking about her, about what happened, tends to make the world around me disappear.

Muttering my thanks, I hang up on Spencer before I back out of the deal. I need to pack my battle armor because I'm headed to war. My head and my heart have been fighting each other for years, and this weekend will be no different. If anything, the battle will intensify.

My phone chimes in my hand minutes later with an incoming message. True to his word, Spencer has sent me not only a confirmation for my reservation at the Hideaway but also an itinerary. I need to buy a plane ticket and start packing. My schedule this week was already light because of the significance of Saturday. Knowing I tend to break down the day before, I was prepared.

I found that out the hard way. In front of my boss. The tears wouldn't stop. I couldn't catch my breath long enough to explain why I was crying.

Still, this throws a hiccup in my already modified work schedule this week. I'll need to cancel an interview on Wednesday afternoon—so I can catch a flight—and clear my schedule Thursday.

Sending my assistant an email, I attach the itinerary and ask her to adjust accordingly and book me a flight for as early in the afternoon as possible. With the time change, I'll already be losing three hours. I'd rather not be checking into my room in the middle of the night. An hour later, I'm staring at my partially packed suitcases, a feeling of uncertainty washing over me.

I can't do this. I can't go back there. What the hell was I thinking agreeing to this?

I'm considering texting Spencer an apology when an

email from my assistant with my flight information and modified schedule comes through. There's no changing my mind now. This is happening.

I'm returning to Great Falls for the first time since I ran, almost five years ago. I swore I'd never go back. One bad memory overshadows all the good. And it's that memory that's the very reason for my return.

To honor my friend.

To celebrate her life.

To remember who she was before she was taken from us.

Because of me.

two

ONE STEP AT A TIME.

That's what I kept telling myself this morning while I finished packing, shoving the bare essentials in my suitcase as it taunted me. Those same words were on repeat as I mindlessly drove to my only scheduled interview of the day where I took subpar notes that I'll more than likely have to review more than once when I get back. And they were still my focus as my assistant drove me to the airport.

When she asked me what was in Tennessee, I couldn't come up with a plausible lie, so I spilled the entire story. From starting college, falling for a man who wasn't mine, and finally, Sam's death and the significance of this weekend. Not a single tear fell the entire time I spoke. I kept my emotions on lockdown.

Pushed the tears away.

Forced myself to remain numb to the pain that was etched on my heart.

After Spencer's call, the full weight of this weekend slapped me across the face. My emotions made me feel like I was standing on the ledge, ready to fall to my death at any given moment, but I vowed I wasn't going to cry. I would make good on my promise—return to Great Falls, go through the motions, and allow myself to fall apart as soon as I was home. In the safety of my own apartment. Behind closed doors. Where no one could see me.

But this weekend? I was going to be strong. I was going to guard my heart and remain emotionless. If I allowed myself to feel, I feared I would shatter into pieces and never be able to put myself back together again.

It took me years to reach a point where I didn't dream about that morning. About the phone call that changed everything or the guilt I still carry with me over the events leading up to Sam's death.

The plane ride was a blur. Four hours of pushing away the memories that were trying to assault me. Keeping the fear at bay of reuniting with my friends. Facing them after running without saying good-bye.

But most of the memories were of Sam. Of her contagious smile. The way she used to twist the colorful ends of her hair around her finger while she talked about something that excited her. Or anything really because life was an adventure in her eyes.

There were other moments that kept trying to invade my thoughts, though. Holidays and birthdays. Parties, sleepovers, and camping. The first time I met Spencer. Moving into my apartment across the parking lot from him and Jay.

Jay.

His name alone causes my heart to race. The very thought of seeing him again makes my body hum with anticipation and dread. It's been five years, yet I still remember the way it felt to be held in his arms. The way his mouth would curve into a smile against my lips right before he kissed me.

Spencer said I was the last to agree. That everyone was going to be there this weekend.

We were going to do this together.

Will Jay be there? I can only assume, but now I'm wishing I had asked Spencer directly.

The urge to run away again is overwhelming. Not just from the events of the upcoming weekend, but from the reminder of the weeks and months leading up to Sam's death, from Jay and the butterflies that only make their presence known when I think of him. When I dream of him.

I can only imagine the flutter I'll feel if I see him again. Hurricane force winds.

If I was going to turn around and head home with my tail tucked between my legs, I should have done it before now. My friends are expecting me to be there for them tomorrow morning. It's a little late to change my mind. Especially with the city limit sign taunting me.

Welcome to Great Falls!

A small town with a rich history.

When I spot it in the distance my hands begin to shake, my grip on the steering wheel tightening as I force myself to pull over. Another five hundred feet and I'll be in the place where my life fell apart. I've come this far, there's no turning back now. I know this, yet I can't seem to shift my rental car into drive. Or get the shaking to stop. Focus on anything except what lies ahead of me.

Lies.

Guilt.

Death.

The aftermath.

A celebration of the life that was taken.

I've spent the last three days dreading this moment. Contemplating canceling but unable to make the call knowing I 'would let Spencer down. And Mia. And

Summer. Everyone. I'd like to think I'm not afraid of much considering what I do for a living, yet a small town in the middle of nowhere Tennessee scares the crap out of me.

Once I cross the invisible line in front of me, I know it's all going to come back full force. The first time I visited here. How excited I was to finally be on my own, in college, far away from the hustle and bustle of Los Angeles. Away from my parents and their upturned noses.

The fact they didn't approve of my choice in universities was part of the draw. I knew they'd never come to visit. The nearest airport is over an hour away and Great Falls doesn't offer five-star hotel accommodations.

And I was right. They never visited.

Not when my best friend was brutally murdered.

Not when I walked across the auditorium stage and received my degree.

Not even to help me pack up the life I had built and return home.

Not once did they step foot here in the four years I spent making this tiny town my home. A town I thought was safe until one night it no longer was. Where everyone knows everything, yet no one saw or heard anything when Sam was murdered. A place I thought I would never leave.

Until the day my grip on reality slipped through my fingers and shattered on the ground. I've picked up most of the pieces, but left behind a huge part of myself when I drove away that rainy late-April morning.

I came here an optimist. Anything was possible. My life was mine to mold. I could achieve every goal I set for myself as long as I put in the work.

The reality that life was fragile never crossed my mind. All I wanted was my freedom and the ability to build the future I'd been dreaming about for years. One where I was my doing what I loved, no matter if my parents approved or not.

A life I now have but feels less perfect than I had imagined. The life I can't get back to until I face what's in front of me.

You can do this.

It's only a few days.

Letting out an audible sigh, I steer the car back on the road and pray for strength.

The town looks exactly as I remember it. The sign for the bowling alley, Lucky Strike, is still only partially lit, the last two letters dark against the setting sun. The theater appears to be playing reruns of old favorites instead of the latest blockbusters according to the marque. And Main Street has the same storefronts from all those years ago, including the Java Bean Coffeehouse, a place I spent many hours studying and visiting my best friend while she worked.

It's not until after I take a right that I realize I'm heading to my old apartment out of habit instead of the Old Town Hideaway B&B where I'm staying. When the apartment complex comes into view, my hands begin to tremble.

Did they ever stop?

So many good memories laced with bad ones.

Parties at Spencer and Jay's place. Sam and I kicking their asses at beer pong. Moving the couch to the parking lot on warm, summer nights so we could be comfortable as we watched the guys play street hockey. Mia gifting Spencer a stripper pole for his birthday and installing it in his bedroom, only to have it rip a giant hole in the ceiling the first time she tried to use it.

My favorite memory will always be of the day I moved in, though.

Before life became complicated.

I lived in the dorms the first two years and was ready for a place of my own after getting stuck with catty roommates. Girls who only cared about themselves, and no matter how nice they were to your face, talked shit about you behind your back. They expected me to be a part of their little circle at first based only on what little they knew about me.

From California. Thin, blonde, and busty.

Of course, all that added up to me being fake like them. They couldn't have been more wrong. Which made my first year in the dorms hell, and the second only slightly better after being assigned a new roommate who was also part of their group.

In a hurry to get away from everything those girls represented, I didn't pack as well as I should have. Most of my things were tossed in random boxes. The lids weren't taped shut. Some were heavy while others were light as a feather. The worst were the ones that were weighted to one side.

I was attempting to carry one of those when I tripped on the curb as I lifted my foot to step onto the sidewalk. A set of strong arms caught me before I hit the ground, but my box didn't fair as well. Underwear and books tumbled across the sidewalk, my face heating in embarrassment.

When I finally righted myself, I came face-to-face with the most stunning pair of hazel eyes. Light toward the edges with dark blue specs around his irises. His woodsy smell would have held me in a trance all on its own if his eyes hadn't been piercing me.

I'm pretty sure I fell in love at first sight that day. My

heart began pounding in my chest, begging to be freed as my lungs struggled to suck in even the tiniest of breaths.

Jay.

The man who would ultimately become my downfall. My one weakness. He could bring me to my knees with just a look, and he did on numerous occasions. Each time making me feel guiltier than the last because he wasn't mine.

I shouldn't have been thinking about him. Fantasizing about his strong arms wrapped around me. Dreaming of him at night when I closed my eyes.

He belonged to Sam.

My new best friend.

The girl I met at work only weeks earlier and hit it off with. The girl who was coming over to help me unpack that night after her shift.

I didn't know he was *her* Jay at the time. I didn't even know his name until two days later. Which is why it's one of my favorite memories. The feelings I felt were still pure. They weren't laced with jealousy as they would be in the following months and years.

In the sixty seconds we spent together, his arms wrapped around me, gently cradling my body against his, the world around us disappeared. The butterflies in my stomach were flapping their wings. My heart was pounding against my chest, begging to be freed. To be given to a man I didn't know. A man who wasn't even asking for it.

So I did.

Metaphorically. I pulled my beating heart from my body, placed it in his hands, and smiled. I'd never been in love before, didn't realize what I was doing. It was reckless, but between the way he was looking at me and the way my body was starting to shake in his arms, it was the only thing that felt right.

I should have been more guarded. Or at least asked him his name. That would have been a better start. Instead, I thanked him and quickly picked up all my panties, rushing into my apartment.

Pushing the memory away, it having soured in my mouth, I turn around in the parking lot, avoiding looking directly at either of our apartments, and head back toward town. I follow Main Street, my eyes focused straight ahead so I don't accidentally glance in the direction of the park. When I turn on 2nd Street, my focus is on Riley's Pub. My old stomping grounds. The only place I spent more time at other than the Java Bean or my apartment.

The place I met Sam. Where our friendship was formed.

The last place she was seen alive.

Averting my eyes, I keep them focused on the road ahead. With the park on one side and Riley's on the other, I can feel the walls around my heart starting to crack. I haven't even been back for twenty minutes and I'm already close to breaking.

It's not until I'm safely behind closed doors in my room at the Hideaway that I let the first and only tear fall. I promised myself I wasn't going to be an emotional wreck this weekend and I plan to try my best to keep that promise. Crying won't bring her back. It won't bring me any peace. All it does is make me appear weak … not that I've done anything to prove how strong I am since my conversation with Spencer.

Hell, I was on the verge of breaking down that night. Instead, I drank an entire bottle of vintage red wine and passed out on my couch. The next morning was a flurry of activity as I arrived late to my first appointment and set myself behind for the rest of the day. By the time I was crawling into bed that night, thoughts of Sam and my impending trip had been long forgotten. Until I spotted my open suitcase sitting partially packed in the corner.

The floodgates opened, and I fell asleep with fresh tears still staining my cheeks. And there she was, in my dream, smiling at me.

Tuesday wasn't much better, and today has been a nightmare. It feels like an elephant has been sitting on my chest since I woke up.

Yet here I am. Riding the emotional rollercoaster that I've been avoiding for the last five years.

The phone in the room rings, and I stare at it for a long moment before quickly crossing the room and answering it. Who has a landline anymore? It's not a hotel. There isn't a need for each room to have a phone. They could easily walk up the single flight of stairs and knock on my door. The entire place only has six room.

"Yes?"

"Andrea? It's Ruth from the kitchen. Since you'll be here for a few days, I was wondering if there was anything special you'd like me to prepare for you. We serve break-fast and lunch but you'll be on your own for dinner."

The sincerity in her voice reminds me of small-town life. A place where you're treated with respect until you do something to lose it. Where everyone knows your name and it feels like you're part of one large family.

"No, thank you. Whatever you have planned will be delicious I'm sure."

In all honestly, I have no appetite right now. All I want are a pair of yoga pants, an over-sized sweatshirt, and a good book. Two of those things can happen but the book will have to wait. I have notes and reports to sort through before I can read for pleasure. I need to try and make sense of today's interview or I'll start forgetting details.

After quickly changing, I head down to the main living area. It doesn't offer much—a couch, two chairs, and a self-service coffee station—but it's quiet and cozy. That's more than I'd get from a fancy hotel.

This place has an antique feel to it. It's been remodeled over the years but it still holds the classic charm you find in historic homes, from the archways and crown molding to the rich colors of the wood. There's a stone fireplace in the corner of the living room that is burning, the wood crackling softly. The mantel above it is straight out of a home magazine and would be perfect for hanging stocking at Christmas.

My room holds the same charm. A four-poster bed sits in the middle of the room, flanked on either side by a dark wood matching table, topped with gorgeous lamps with cream-colored shades that match the curtains. There's a roll-top desk along one wall and a dresser along the other. What I'm assuming used to be a closet has been converted into a small, private bathroom.

The walls are adorned in bright artwork, bringing out the colors of the knit blanket on the bed. They're more modern than the rest of the room but the tarnished gold frames tie it all together.

Setting my bag on the couch, I walk over to the coffee station. With trembling hands, I pop a pod into the machine, my finger lingering over the brew button for a moment. The little green light blinks at me, taunting me.

I should have stocked up on iced coffee.

I can handle this. It's just one cup. Plus, I need it or I'll fall asleep and be even further behind on work.

Once I've doctored my coffee so it tastes more like sugar and creamer than actual roasted beans, I curl up on the couch and retrieve my paperwork from my satchel. The place is eerily silent, which doesn't surprise me. Great Falls isn't a tourist town. Unless it's the start of the school year or graduation, I can't imagine either of the two B&B's are ever fully booked.

Which makes this the perfect place to focus on work and avoid thinking about why I'm really here. An attempt to keep the memories at bay, at least for the night. Tomorrow is a different story. According to my itinerary, Spencer and I have a meeting with the dean at Great Falls University. I have no idea what it's about, but I know it has something to do with Sam and that's enough to make me uneasy.

The university is hosting a memorial brunch Friday afternoon and a lantern release on Friday night. As much as I would love to skip both of those events, I have a feeling Spence would hunt me down if I didn't show up. Not to mention, Friday will be easy compared to what the town has planned for Saturday.

The actual anniversary of Sam's death.

It starts with the first annual Samantha Bridges 5k marathon. It's been years since I've run outside, let alone more than a mile or two. The marathon isn't what scares me, though. It's what happens after everyone is done running.

The fountain dedication.

In the park.

Where Sam was killed.

On the anniversary of her death.

A permanent reminder of the tragedy. In the very place it happened.

I haven't been back to the park since that night. I avoided it at all costs the last few months I lived here and now I'm expected to what? Just walk in the park like it's no big deal? Like what happened that night didn't alter me in a way I still haven't recovered from?

One step at a time.

My new personal mantra, because if I look too far ahead, I'm going to shatter without warning. No amount of glue will be able to piece me back together this time.

three

SLEEP DIDN'T COME EASY. BETWEEN THE TIME DIFFERENCE and the two cups of coffee I ended up drinking, it was close to three o'clock before I was finally able to crawl in bed. Once I was about to drift off to sleep, I heard a noise. The floor creaked as if someone was standing outside of my door. The thought alone caused my adrenaline to soar.

Which is why I'm standing outside of the Java Bean right now, debating on going inside. I had two cups of coffee with the omelet Ruth made me this morning, but they didn't even faze me. I could have drunk an entire pot of coffee and I have a feeling I would have been able to fall back asleep no problem. Still, a double-shot vanilla latte with skim milk sounds amazing right now. Extra-large. Maybe two. More than anything, it's necessary if I want to make it through the meeting I have with the dean in less than thirty minutes.

Going inside brings with it a new set of emotions, though. Emotions I'm not sure I'm strong enough to handle on the little sleep I was able to get. Memories that will tear me apart and bring me back to a time I've tried to bury down deep because I'm not sure I'll even be able to handle reliving them.

"You gonna stare at her through the window all day or go inside and say hello?"

Letting out a sigh, I turn to face the familiar voice even though I'm not entirely sure I'm ready. This weekend is already starting to feel like I'm ripping off band-aid after band-aid. Reopening wounds that have never fully healed. Wounds I've tried to ignore instead of deal with.

"Spencer," I say, walking into his open arms. When they wrap around me in a warm embrace, a single tear falls.

Damn it.

I promised I was going to keep myself in check. Yet, my damn tears didn't seem to get the memo. I blame the lack of sleep.

He feels the same as I remember. His large body has always made me feel safe though the first time I met him, I was slightly intimidated. He had shaved his head bald after losing a bet. Between his size, his shiny new dome, and the leather jacket he was wearing, he looked like he was in a biker gang. All that was missing was the motorcycle.

One conversation was all it took for me to realize I had judged a book by its cover. He was sweet and cuddly. More like a teddy bear, even without the hair. He never took himself or anything seriously. When he wasn't cracking jokes, he was dancing around like a fool or poking fun at us girls. His teasing was relentless. He always found a way to use our words against us. Mainly turning any normal comment into a sexual innuendo.

When I would stay up late studying and complain, *"I didn't get enough sleep last night."*

His response would always be, *"Who was the lucky guy?"*

If I was talking to Mia about needing my hair done and say something along the lines of, *'My hair's a mess."*

He would respond with, *'Who was pulling on it?"*

After working all night, I'd plop down on their couch

and throw my feet up on the table with Sam by my side. One of us would always say, '*My feet hurt.*'

Spencer's comeback? '*You mean your knees? We're you down on them again?*'

After a while, you could almost anticipate what he was going to say. Still, there were times he would surprise me by offering to rub my feet or brush my hair instead of making a witty remark. Or the time he came home with three little foot spas and set them out for us girls, pampering us for a few hours.

"It's good to see you, Andi. I missed you, my California beauty queen." I can hear the sincerity in his words as he squeezes me tightly, holding me pressed against his chest.

Smiling against his shirt, I can't help but giggle at the ridiculous nickname he gave me the first time we met. I had hoped it wouldn't stick but it did. However, he wouldn't let anyone use it. Not even Jay, his best friend and roommate. Though he did on more than one occasion to piss Spencer off. Usually when we were all good and drunk.

Always after Spencer and I beat him and Sam at beer pong.

"I missed you, too, Spence," I admit, taking a step back as he holds me at arm's length. "You look exactly the same. How is that possible? Do you not age?"

"I can't give away all my secrets," he replies with a smirk.

"Mia's been making you use those creams on your face, hasn't she?" I tease, knowing damn well there's a strong possibility it's actually true. Before he can deny it, I change the subject. "Where is Mia?"

"Working, per usual. I promised her we'd stop by after

our meeting so she could see you but now I'm reconsidering." Spencer taps his finger against his lips as if he's thinking hard about the decision. As if he really has a choice. Regardless, I'll play along.

"What? Why?" I ask, the bell above the Java Bean door startling me as a middle-aged man comes barreling out.

"Don't take this the wrong way, but you look like shit, Andi. Did you even sleep last night?" I can hear the concern in his voice laced with mock horror.

"I think the Hideaway is haunted. I kept hearing footsteps outside of my door, so no, I didn't get much sleep," I confess as I tuck a stray curl behind my ear, averting my gaze.

"Which means you need coffee yet you're standing out here instead of in there."

All I can do is nod, my eyes still focused on the bike rack behind him as the bell chimes again, but I don't notice anyone walk past us this time. I don't have to wait long to find out why when a pair of skinny arms wrap around me from behind at the same time lips are pressed against my cheek.

"The second child returns home," Summer announces excitedly, releasing me from her hold as she throws her hands in the air. Sliding up next to me, she turns her attention to Spence and winks. "I really thought you were lying to me, Spencer."

"You think so little of me after everything I've done for you. I still don't understand." His mocking tone tells me he understands completely why she doesn't trust him.

The pranks we all used to play on Summer are legendary. Everyone in town would talk about them, some offering suggestions for next time while others were oblivious to the fact that we were the ones behind them.

They weren't always elaborate. We'd move things around in the shop after she closed for the night. Flip the menus so they were hanging upside down. Change the prices of everything either up or down depending on our mood.

My favorite pranks were always the ones that revolved around decorating for the holidays. If it was Easter, we'd hang Halloween decorations. For Christmas, Independence Day decor. They never matched the actual holiday, and after a few seasons, Summer gave up buying decorations at all knowing that someone was going to foil her plans. It was a surprise to her when she walked in to work on Valentine's Day and everything was pink and red and white. Giant hearts were hanging from the ceiling and there were window clings of little cupids. She always blamed Spencer for being the mastermind behind them when really it was Sam.

Valentine's Day was the last holiday we decorated the shop.

It was also Sam and Jay's anniversary.

The combination of the two reasons are why I never celebrate it. Why I don't like celebrating any holidays I can avoid. Most of my best memories were made with a girl who isn't here anymore. With friends I haven't spoken to in years. The holidays serve as reminders of what I had and lost in the blink of an eye.

"So I can tell at least one of you needs a strong cup of coffee," Summer says, wrapping her arm around my waist and pulling me against her like old times. She barely comes up to my chin, standing a little under five foot tall, so I automatically sling my arm over her shoulder.

Sam was the spitting image of her mother. Short in stature with a personality larger than life. Light brown, straight hair with dark, muddy brown eyes. Where Sam was curvier in the hips and thighs, Summer has always been petite. Looking at her today, she appears thinner than I remember her being. Not unhealthy but more fragile.

I imagine we all are, either on the inside or out.

Spencer holds the door for us as we make our way inside, Summer slipping behind the counter. The sounds and smells of the Java Bean take me back. To a time when life was simple. When I used to sit at the table in the corner and stare out the window when I was supposed to be studying. When Sam and I would cuddle up on the couch in front of the fireplace and talk while the snow fell outside.

We 'would make plans for when the weather warmed. Sam had a list of epic adventures she longed to take. Places she craved to visit, things she needed to see and experience. The ocean was at the top of her list. She said it was so vast it scared her. Made her feel even smaller and she was hell-bent on conquering every fear she had.

Mostly, this place reminds me of the last morning I saw her. Her hair was piled on top of her head in a messy bun, the bright teal tips sticking out in every direction. She had my mocha waiting for me and a sad smile on her face, her bright red lipstick emphasizing her mood. Her eyes were pleading with me not to go, but all I could think about was how I needed to get away from that place and clear my head. To put distance between me and Jay before we crossed a line. Again.

Sure, I was excited to lay on the beach and soak up the sun, but it wasn't the real reason I was rushing off that morning. I was going on an all-expenses paid vacation to St. Lucia with my parents. Their favorite vacation destination. An early graduation gift. My days would be spent drinking on the beach and listening to the waters of the Caribbean lap against the sand. At night my parents wanted to show me their favorite sights on the island.

Four nights and five days of relaxation.

It was my last semester of college. I was exhausted and needed the vacation. I'd been counting down the days until spring break for months. My car was packed, and I was on my way to the airport.

I barely said hello and good-bye to her that morning at she handed me my mocha, the guilt gnawing at my soul. If I'd known then what I know now, I would have hugged her tighter. Told her how important she was to me.

Hell, I probably would've stayed in Great Falls and spent spring break with her. Faced the consequences of my actions for a few more days with her.

"Here ya go," I hear Spencer say from next to me.

When I glance in his direction, I find his outstretched hand with a paper cup in it. "I didn't order anything."

"Summer made you a mocha with an extra shot. She said the sugar and caffeine would get you going."

All I can do is nod as I take the cup from him and bring it to my lips, blowing air through the opening in the lid as I take another look around the shop. It hasn't changed. Same furniture. Same setup. Same everything.

I'm starting to wonder if time has stood still in Great Falls. At least for some people.

Spencer is quiet on the walk through campus. I keep my eyes focused straight ahead until we're seated outside of the dean's office, not wanting more memories to assault me. I'm already feeling fragile, like an emotional bomb waiting to explode.

Tick. Tick. Tick.

"The dean will see you now," a hunched-over older lady says, appearing out of nowhere.

The dean is situated behind his desk as Spencer and I enter. He motions for us to take a seat without looking away from his computer. After a few long, tense moments, he removes his wire-rimmed glasses, tosses them on his desk, and runs his fingers through his graying hair.

"Thank you both for coming in today. The university is pleased to be a part of Sam's remembrance. She was an excellent student and a leader in the community. It's a tragedy what happened to her, and what you've put together is inspiring." His attention is solely focused on Spencer even though it's clear he's talking to both of us. "We have the foyer of the student center set up to host the memorial brunch tomorrow afternoon, and the lantern release will be on the football field at dusk. With this week being spring break, most of our student population is off campus. However, we've had a number of community members RSVP for one or both events along with many of our student leaders returning to campus tonight and tomorrow morning. The only thing we haven't secured is a speaker for the lantern release."

The room falls silent as both Spencer and the dean stare at me expectantly.

"I can't."

Two words. That's all I get out. There are a million reasons running through my mind, but none of them feel validated.

"Your excuses are lame." Spencer rolls his eyes at me. "I'm already kicking off the 5k race on Saturday, and Summer is speaking at the fountain dedication after. It would mean a lot to both of us if you could speak at the lantern release."

I open my mouth to protest but nothing comes out. Which is what scares me most about speaking in front of a crowd. Especially about Sam. And if the words won't come, the tears will. The last thing I want is to have an emotional breakdown in front of half the town.

"If you won't do it for us, do it for Sam," Spencer urges. Not only was that a low blow but he's flaunting his signature pout.

I have no idea how Mia is able to say no to him when he pulls this shit. I swear, the 'puppy dog' look has never worked on me before, except when it came to Spence. Probably because he doesn't use it all the time. Only when something matters to him, and I know this does.

Because Sam mattered to him. She mattered to all of us. She was the glue that kept us all together. Which is probably why I feel like my heart is still in pieces.

"Fine, but I want to be behind the crowd. I don't want to stand in front of anyone. I don't want people staring at me. And I can't promise how long I'll be able to talk about her, but I'll try."

"Thank you, Andrea. It's never easy to talk about the people we've loved and lost, but knowing Sam for as long as I have, as long as I did, I think she would be pleased," the dean remarks as he stands.

Damn small-town politics.

Stupid everyone-knows-everyone place.

I should have seen this coming. The itinerary Spencer sent was detailed. I knew he was speaking at the race, and Summer at the dedication. What I didn't notice was the lack of a speaker at the lantern release.

"She would be pleased, you know," Spencer adds as we walk back across campus toward Main Street.

Sam would be happier if she were still alive.

I want to say the words, they're on the tip of my tongue, but they're filled with spite. I haven't seen Spencer in almost five years and the last thing I want to do is fight with him the entire time I'm here.

Or worse, ruin our friendship. I can't take another loss right now.

four

I WOULDN'T BE SURPRISED IF MIA'S SCREECH WAS HEARD IN the next town over. The shrill sound of her voice caused me to cringe even though I was actually happy to see her. She was bouncing in her heels when she spotted Spencer and I walking into Blush, the salon she's been working at since I've known her. Then she was sprinting toward me, the click of her heels the only warning I was given as she launched herself at me.

"I've missed you so much," she says enthusiastically, throwing her arms around my neck as the three women seated in the waiting area, all a decade older than us, watch in fascination. "I can't believe you've stayed away this long. How could you not visit?"

Slapping me in the arm when she finally releases me, Mia steps back and wrinkles her nose, getting a good look at me for the first time. Spence warned me I looked like shit, not that I wasn't aware before he so sweetly pointed it out.

"You look like hell, Andi. Well, your hair is gorgeous as always, but this …" Mia waves her hand in front of my face before continuing, "this needs some help. You need some under eye cream to get rid of those puffy bags and maybe a little Botox to help with your crow's feet. They're not horrifying yet, but if you don't start taking better care of your skin they will be in a few years."

"I'm twenty-seven, Mia, not seventy. I don't think I have to worry about crow's feet just yet."

One of the women in the waiting area scoffs at my remark, but I don't bother to acknowledge it.

Mia hasn't changed a bit. Still bubbly. Still smiling. Her ginger curls are pulled into a fashionable rat's nest on the top of her head, tendrils framing her face.

She's always been gorgeous and she knows it. As a stylist, she's found ways to accent her best features and her talent has only grown with time. The dark and often dramatic eye makeup she used to wear is gone, in it's place more neutral tones that bring out the sandy color of her eyes. Her fair skin is dusted with bronzer, accenting her high cheekbones. Her pouty lips have been glossed with a hue of pink and nothing more.

Her words cut through the haze that was beginning to consume me as I admired her beautiful features.

"Have you looked in a mirror recently?" she asks, astonished that I would doubt her.

Of course I have. In fact, I looked this morning before I left to meet Spencer and cringed, adding more concealer under my eyes in a vain attempt to hide the dark circles. I even took my hair out of the high ponytail I had it in so it framed my face.

"I try really hard not to sometimes," I mutter as she turns and heads toward the back of the salon, stopping at her station to snag a few products she has sitting on the counter.

"Let's go," Spencer says, nudging me with his shoulder before taking my hand in his and tugging until my feet cooperate.

"Where?" I ask as we leave the buzz of hairdryers behind us.

"Lunch. Mia put your favorite in the oven this morning and it should be ready."

Following Mia and Spencer through the salon and then up the familiar set of stairs, I'm surprised to find their loft has been fully remodeled. When they moved in together during our senior year, the place was nice enough but needed a little work. Fresh paint and floors would have gone a long way. From the looks of it, they did that and more.

The kitchen has been completely transformed from a galley style with a half wall and the dining room separating it from the living room to an open concept. Shiny new appliances in black stainless steel, soft white, granite countertops, and heather gray cabinets. The island that replaced the half wall now separates the kitchen from the dining area and matches the rest of the kitchen with the exception of the cabinets. They're painted a darker shade of gray, making them stand out against the stark white counters.

The shaggy, yellowing carpet I was afraid to walk on has been replaced with oak wood floors. The walls are painted a shade of gray so soft it's almost white, complementing the color scheme in the kitchen.

The living room would be boring if it weren't for the pops of color everywhere. Dark blue throw pillows that match the curtains accent a large, red sectional. Bright, abstract paintings are on every wall. White tables and a matching entertainment center with a large, flat screen TV hanging above it brighten the area.

And then there's my least favorite showpiece sitting in the far corner of the room, taunting me.

The teal chair my parents bought me for my apartment

for Christmas. I hated that chair from the moment it showed up at my door. Now, I resent it. It's the chair that inspired Sam to change the color in her hair.

"You kept it?" I ask, sliding onto a bar stool at the island without taking my eyes off the chair. My question isn't directed at either of them in particular, but Spencer was the one who wanted it.

"Of course we did. I love that damn chair. It's uncomfortable as hell and no one ever sits in it, but it looks great," Spencer replies, proud of the eye sore.

"It's ugly as sin, Spencer." Turning in my seat, I find both of them staring at me in utter amusement. "I can't believe you let him talk you into keeping it, Mia. I gave it to him as a joke."

After Sam's death, the chair haunted me. I tried to smash it with a baseball bat but I wasn't strong enough to break it. The damn thing was expensive and apparently made well. Eventually, I asked Spencer to take it out of my apartment. I figured he was joking when he asked if he could have it.

"I'll admit, I think it's horrendous. Spence is the only one who likes it, but something feels wrong about getting rid of it, so instead we let it inspire the remodel."

Glancing around the room, I can see that everything is brought together by the chair. The colors, the styles. The damn chair is the centerpiece of the design. Somehow, they managed to have a completely unique and beautiful apartment and incorporate that ugly-ass chair.

Mia dishes out her homemade macaroni and cheese, and we fall into easy conversation. The remodel of the loft. The fights they had over every detail. Mia buying the salon from the previous owner last year when she decided to retire.

Nothing they say shocks me until Spencer gets a phone call from his boss.

The chief of police.

"Spence is a police officer?" I ask Mia in hushed tones as Spencer paces the living room.

Spencer was studying criminal justice. It's not a stretch that he became a police officer, but he had always talked about going to law school. I envisioned him in the courtroom, his larger-than-life stature intimidating everyone until he opened his mouth.

"He went into the academy shortly after you left and was promoted to detective last year," she explains, avoiding eye contact.

"Is he looking into Sam's death?" I ask, already knowing the answer.

"When he can. There have been no new leads, no breaks in the case, so they're going to close it soon."

No. They can't. They need to find whoever did this to her. It's not fair. Sam deserves justice. We deserve closure.

Anger begins to bubble beneath the surface, but I tamp it down. Getting worked up isn't going to solve anything. It's not going to make this weekend easier. Plus, I already went through that stage of grieving. I'm stuck on the final stage. Acceptance.

Clearing my mind, I let what Mia said sink in before composing myself and opening my eyes to the bigger picture. What is going on this weekend. Why I'm here.

"It's why he was pushing me to come back and get closure because he knows I'd be notified that the case was officially closed." Mia nods, tears glistening in the corner of her eyes. "I don't know if I can do this, Mia. Being here again is hard. Don't get me wrong. I missed you guys. I'm glad I got the chance to see you, but I don't know if I can stay. It's too hard. It hurts too much."

"Don't run away again, Andi. I get it, I really do, but I don't think Spence really understands how you could walk away and never look back. Sam's death changed all of us. He ran toward it, jumped in, wanting to do whatever he could to help." She pauses, looking down to where her hands are clasped together in front of her. "Jay, too."

"Jay?" I ask, his name coming out raspier than I anticipated.

The mention of his names causes my breath to hitch, my heart to race, and goosebumps to cover my arms. I still don't know if he's going to be here this weekend. I want to ask but I press my lips together instead, silencing myself. Saying his name was hard enough.

"Yeah. He went to the academy, too, only he was recruited to work for the government shortly after graduating. Something to do with security clearance and his degree. He can't really say. I know his dad has some major pull but I'm not sure what. The plan was for both of them to stay here and work Sam's case when they could. Jay left, and Spence was left to pick up the pieces all by himself.

"So, if you stay for no other reason than for Spencer, that's fine. But please understand that he needs you right now. We all do. We've been facing this every day for the last five years and it's about to be over. When that happens, it'll be easier for everyone if we're together."

Together.

It's the confirmation I need. Jay will be here this weekend. So, we can all say our final goodbyes as a united front. We'll face it together, like we did when she died. Only this time, five years have passed, and we don't really know each other anymore.

"I ..."

Words fail me as I stare into Mia's pleading green eyes. More than anything, I want to confess all the things she doesn't know. About what happened before Sam died. The secrets I've kept from all of them since leaving here. The fact that I, too, ran toward helping Sam, only I haven't found the answers yet.

I didn't want to say anything until I had information that could help.

And I don't, which makes me feel like a complete failure.

"It's okay," Mia replies with the shake of her head as Spencer slides back onto his bar stool, tossing his phone on the counter. "What's wrong, babe? You look frustrated."

"The chief wants me to come down and sign the official paperwork to close Sam's case." Spencer chances a glance in my direction but avoids eye contact. I can see the weight on his shoulders growing heavier by the second. Closing Sam's case will be a double-edged sword for him.

Same as it will for me.

The failure will outweigh the relief of having to relive that night over and over again.

"It's your birthday. You're on vacation this week. Did you tell him it would have to wait until Monday?"

Birthday? Shit. How could I forget?

"Yeah, and he's not happy. He knows I'm in town. He knows what this weekend is. He thinks it would be better to close it now and announce that it's closed at the dedication."

The room falls silent as we all soak in the reality of Spencer's statement. Confessing to the entire town that the person who murdered Sam has gotten off scot-free. That they'll never be caught because we're giving up.

No. I can't let that happen. It's not right. We can do better. Sam deserves better.

"It wouldn't. Be better to do it at the fountain dedication, I mean." My words are barely above a whisper but they're strong. Confident. If only my voice would sound it. "Let me talk to him."

"He's not going to listen to you, Andi. He's a stubborn bastard." Spencer lets out a guttural growl, and then slams his fist against the counter in frustration.

"Yeah, but maybe I can stall him," I state, standing. Both of them stare at me in confusion, as they should. "I work for the State of California, but he can grant me special privileges here in Tennessee. I'm a criminal profiler. I interview and study the behavior of criminals after they're caught. I analyze every detail of their crimes from their choice of weapon to their method of attack. I study their personalities, what aspects of their life made them the way they are, and create a profile. We use those profiles to help catch other criminals. Maybe I can stall him by offering my services. If he agrees, I could put together a profile for your team to use. It's a last-ditch effort, but if it helps, I'd be willing to put one together. It normally takes me more than a few days but I could try."

"You interview criminals?" is all Spencer asks after a few seconds.

"Yeah. From serial killers to car thieves and everything in between. The goal is to get to a point where we can predict what a person will do next based on their previous behavior and prevent it from happening."

"And I thought a degree in psychology was going to be a waste of time," Mia adds, stabbing a few noodles of her forgotten macaroni and shoving them in her mouth. Her words are muffled, more than likely on purpose, as she says, "I can admit I was wrong."

"Shall we go have a talk with your boss?" I ask Spencer, who's still currently staring at me wide-eyed with his mouth hanging open in shock.

After thanking Mia for lunch and promising to meet her for dinner that night, Spencer and I walk the three blocks to the Great Falls City Complex. It houses the police and fire stations as well as the courthouse and city offices. Basically, all the government offices are crammed into the three-story, historic building. In a town this small, that's more than enough space to accommodate every department.

"Happy birthday, by the way," I say as we cross the street.

"Thanks. Not much to celebrate yet."

"Aside from how fantastic you are." I nudge him with my shoulder. "I get that the timing of … everything is a little shitty but don't let that ruin your special day."

"I'll start celebrating my birthday after this is over. Once the asshole is behind bars. Once I know the people of this town can sleep soundly again at night. When people don't have to worry about walking in the park alone after dark. Then and only then will I celebrate today."

The anger in his voice rises with each word. Swallowing past the lump in my throat, I nod my head in acceptance of his answer. If he doesn't want to celebrate, I'm not going to force him.

Our meeting with the chief is short and sweet but not without conflict.

He pressures Spencer to sign the papers to close the case, thrusting them in his hands as soon as we walk in his office.

Spencer refuses, tossing the paperwork on the chief's desk, knocking over an empty coffee cup.

They argue about the merits of making the announcement when the majority of the town is gathered for the ceremony. If I weren't personally affiliated with the case, I'd side with the chief. Telling everyone at the same time will make it easier for some people to take the news. Still, I side with Spencer and explain why, offering my services.

The chief refuses before I can even explain what I want to try and do.

Spencer attempts to make him a deal, agreeing to sign the papers on Monday if he allows me to create a profile. The chief relents after I give him a brief summary of my work over the last four years. How it can potentially help the case. My resume speaks for itself. I've worked some high-profile cases in California. One led to the capture of a serial rapist and the other stopped a potential serial killer. He had his victim, and we were able to save her because of the profile I put together in less than two days.

Which is what I'm going to have to do again. I have roughly seventy-two hours to study Sam's case from beginning to end before I have to present a complete profile to the chief along with Spencer and his team.

"That's impressive, you know," Spencer says as he walks me back to my car that's still parked in front of the Java Bean.

"What is?"

"What you do. Don't get me wrong, I know there's honor and merit in being a police officer, but what you do, getting in the heads of criminals and figuring them out, that's really amazing. Scary at times I'm sure, but amazing nonetheless."

All I can do is nod.

I can't confess I took the job because of Sam. Or that I get creeped out sometimes when I'm alone in a room with someone who's killed twenty people before getting caught. I can't confess I have nightmares more often than not or that in most of those nightmares the victim is always Sam.

five

After parting ways with Spencer, I head back to the Hideaway to do some research before I have to meet up with him and Mia for dinner. Between the files the chief let me borrow currently sitting in my passenger seat and old newspaper articles that covered Sam's death, I should be able to get a good start on my profile.

I need to know how much information was disclosed.

How much the police shared with the town.

What details they kept to themselves; details only the person responsible would know.

I don't remember much of what I was told at the time. My sole focus was blaming myself. I shut myself in my apartment. Stopped taking phone calls after her funeral. Threw myself into the last few weeks of school, and once I graduated, I left. It didn't matter who or how, the outcome was still the same. Sam was gone and I was to blame.

Had I not missed my flight, she wouldn't have been working my shift that night. She wouldn't have been walking home through the park. A place that we'd walked together at night before and never thought twice about our safety.

Had I not gone on spring break she might still be here. We would still be friends. I may never have left Great Falls.

There are a million what-if's I could debate but none of

them change the outcome. No amount of rationalization or beating myself up will bring her back. Because she's gone. Someone murdered her that night, as I was driving home.

I have to focus on the facts of the case.

The evidence.

Leave my personal feelings out of it. Right now, Sam is a victim. Not my best friend. Not the petite girl with the large personality that forced her way into my life after only working one shift together. The girl who loved to dye her hair crazy colors and write with fuzzy-topped pens. Who smelled like coffee all the time and acted like it was pumping through her veins all hours of the day.

Nope.

Right now, she's just a victim.

After setting myself up at the tiny desk in my room, I shoot my personal assistant an email asking for profiles on similar cases. Small town murders. It doesn't take her long to reply, and soon I'm reviewing three cases that are identical to each other. All the suspects were upstanding community members. All caught because they slipped up and left DNA behind.

The one thing I do find helpful is that in all three of those cases, the murderer was organized. He planned and executed practically flawlessly. They were familiar with the area, their victim. Then, when in the act, they got sloppy. They left behind a piece of themselves because they were excited.

After setting those cases aside, I scour through all the articles published on Sam's death, jotting down details and making notes for myself. Questions I need to find answers to. Missing information to look for.

Two hours later, I'm about to open the first of a dozen

police files when the alarm on my cell phones startles me, causing me to drop the folder, the contents spilling everywhere. Quickly gathering all the papers, I'm shoving them back in the file when a picture that slid beneath the desk catches my attention.

Slowly reaching for it, my hand begins to shake as I read what's written on the back.

Samantha Bridges

Crime scene photo #2

I stare at the words scrawled in messy black sharpie for a few minutes before I shove the photo in the folder without looking at it. Quickly grabbing my phone, I shut off the alarm, toss it in my purse, and head out for dinner. My hands are still shaking as I slowly descend the staircase. Brandon Royal and his wife, Ruth, are standing at the front desk, chatting when I walk by. They both smile and wave as I pass, but I can't bring myself to return their greeting. Instead, I rush out the front door, letting it slam behind me.

Once I'm safely behind the wheel of my rental car, I suck in a deep breath and let it out slowly, attempting to calm my racing heart. I knew this was going to be hard. Seeing pictures of Sam. Reliving her murder. I need to turn my emotions off and focus but I can't treat this like any other case. It's not. Not even close.

The drive to the diner feels like hours when it actually takes me less than five minutes. As soon as I walk in, I spot Mia sitting at a booth in the back. Her ginger curls bounce around as she waves at me over her head like it's the first time she's seen me in years instead of hours. She appears just as excited as she did earlier at the salon. The look of sorrow on her face before Spence and I headed to the police station is long gone, replaced with a huge smile and a sparkle in her eye.

Mia's always been brave. Braver than I am. She was the one who tried to help me through the grief when it should have been the other way around. She knew Sam longer. They grew up together and were as close as Sam and I were.

The thought makes me realize what a shitty friend I was after everything happened. Not just to Mia but to Spencer as well. They lost Sam, and then I left them with no concern for their well-being. My sole focus was getting as far away from here as possible in hopes of alleviating the pain.

Not that my plan worked. The pain was just as intense from three-thousand miles away, and instead of being surrounded by people who understood what I was going through, people who were also grieving, I was alone.

"Hey, sorry I'm late. I got caught up in research," I explain as I sit across from her, shaking away the memories of Mia holding me while I cried. "Where's Spencer?"

"He'll be here shortly." Her demeanor shifts suddenly, her response clipped as she averts her eyes, studying the menu in her hand. A menu she more than likely has memorized considering there are only two restaurants in town.

"Something you want to share with me?" I press, nudging her with the toe of my boot under the table.

"Um, no." She glances at me over the menu but it's so brief our eyes barely make contact before she's looking down again.

"You do realize you're a horrible liar, right? You can't make eye contact with me, and the pitch of your voice just went up a few notches. So, I'll ask you again. Anything you want to share with me?"

Letting out a sigh, Mia finally raises her eyes to look at me, only instead of meeting mine, she looks over my left shoulder. I'm about to follow her line of sight when her face lights up again, her mega-watt smile showcasing her perfectly straight, white teeth.

Spencer's here. Great. It's wonderful that she still looks at him like that after all this time. They've been together since I met them my junior year. I'm actually surprised they're not married yet.

"You're here!" Mia screams, bouncing out of her seat.

Turning my entire body expecting to watch Mia jump into Spencer's arms, my jaw drops open when a familiar pair of hazel eyes meet mine at the same moment Mia wraps herself around him. My inhale of breath is barely audible over the beating of my heart. It's the only thing I can hear as I continue to stare at the man who owns my heart.

The same man who was off limits.

Forbidden.

The one man I couldn't have, and the only one I wanted. So I tried to avoid him. When that didn't work, I acted like I could barely stand him. He made that practically impossible. There's no way you couldn't be drawn to him. His personality was magnetic.

I settled for being his friend, which was harder than I anticipated. I didn't trust myself alone with him. Hell, I didn't trust myself to stand next to him in a crowd. I was afraid my true feelings would show. That I'd do something like reach out and take his hand when it wasn't mine to hold.

Basically, I lived on edge whenever he was around for almost two years. Because I couldn't admit to my best friend that I was in love with her boyfriend. Because I didn't want to lose her even though I wanted him.

My eyes are still locked on Jay's as Mia takes him by the elbow and drags him over to the booth. He silently slides in across from me as Mia continues to chatter on in the background.

"You look good, Drea," he finally says, cutting Mia off.

Drea.

He's the only person I've ever let call me that aside from my grandmother.

"Thanks, Jay. You look …" My voice trails off as my brain refuses to feed me a word appropriate enough to describe how delicious he looks.

Time has been good to him. He's always been attractive, but in college his body was still filling out. He spent a lot of time at the gym but he had a runner's body. Strong legs, toned muscles, impressive abs. Fit and trim.

Now he has the body of a god.

His plain black T-shirt is stretched tight across his chest, covering his broad shoulders and defined chest muscles. The corded muscles of his left arm are covered in an intricate tribal tattoo from where his sleeve ends down to his wrist. The black ink against his bronzed skin draws my attention and captures it, making me wonder if he has more artwork hidden beneath his clothes.

Jay lifts his ink-covered arm, brushing his unruly, dark brown hair away from his face, breaking the spell he has on me.

"You were saying?" Mia interjects, a devious smile on her face that clearly says I was caught checking Jay out, as Spencer squeezes my shoulder.

I forgot Mia was even here. *And where did Spencer come*

from? Did he arrive with Jay? And when did he sit down? He's next to me, his arm slung over the back of the booth seat.

"You look different," I finally say, clearing my throat as I attempt to find somewhere to stare except across the table at the gorgeous man who's found a way to render me practically speechless after all this time.

It's not the first time he's managed to do it. It won't be the last. With him this close after all these years, I better get used to communicating without words. Maybe I'll start carrying a dry erase board and markers. Then I'll never have to speak again in his presence. I doubt it would save me from making a fool of myself, though.

Thankfully, the waitress comes over to get our drink order, saving me from having to explain my lame answer.

After ordering, Mia interrogates Jay about what he's been up to since they saw him last, which was only a few months ago. I'm not surprised they've stayed in contact now that I know he went to the academy with Spence.

If I wasn't privy to that information I would have been shocked to know they still talk. He handled Sam's death about as well as I did. He was depressed and blamed himself for not being there. For not protecting her. For not making sure she had a car to drive home that night.

Then he was brought in as a suspect in her death even though he was two hundred miles away when it happened. I remember them interrogating him for hours, trying to get him to confess to something he didn't do. They talked to his boss at Apollo Hardware, co-workers, and friends, trying to find a flaw in his story. His father eventually came to his rescue with a lawyer.

His alibi was solid but the police wanted someone to blame so they could close the case. When they couldn't pin it on Jay, the boyfriend, they started pointing their fingers in other directions. Practically everyone in town was interviewed in the first few weeks. When they ran out of leads, I remember it feeling like they'd given up.

After reading some of the articles this afternoon, I now know why.

There was a lack of evidence left at the scene. No DNA to profile, even though they swabbed everyone when they were interviewed. Not a single hair or fiber found on Sam's body. The rain washed it all away that night.

"Spencer tells me you interview crazy people," I hear Jay say as I pick at the mashed potatoes on my plate with my fork.

"Something like that." I keep my attention focused on my plate, afraid to look in his eyes. To see the surprise. Hell, to see any kind of reaction.

"Don't let her downplay it, man. She psychoanalyzes killers. I have her looking at Sam's case now. Maybe she'll see something we didn't."

We?

Jay looked into Sam's case? I thought he left town.

Would they even let him look at the files after he was a suspect? After meeting the chief, I have a feeling Jay would be blacklisted from getting near the case. He seems like an old-fashioned kind of guy. You know, the one who doesn't like to try new things because the old way has always worked.

"This isn't good dinner conversation," Mia interjects. "Let's talk about something else. Anything."

"Okay," Jay starts, placing his napkin on his empty plate. I've been so focused on spreading my mashed potatoes around my plate I don't even know what he ordered. "You ever going to agree to marry this asshole?"

My head whips in Mia's direction, excepting to see her

roll her eyes, when instead she shrugs her shoulders and smiles. "Maybe one day. He knows what he needs to do before I agree."

"What's that?" I hear myself ask.

"He has to solve Sam's case."

That's a tough request. One I know he wants to honor but if he falls short, if *we* fall short, what then? They continue to live life the way they are now?

"Why?" I ask, astonished that her agreeing to marry Spencer has anything to do with Sam or any case Spence may be working on.

"I've lived here all my life, and when I dreamt of my wedding, I was always married in the park. Right now, it holds bad memories. I can't even bring myself to walk through it. I keep the curtains in the apartment closed and I don't look out the window. Once the case is closed, we'll replace the bad memories with good ones. Right now, it feels like they're lingering.

"These two have worked their asses off to try and find the tiniest break in the case. The longer this goes on, the harder it's going to be to solve. That's why the chief wants to put it to bed. He's given up on solving it but I haven't. Someone knows something, and I won't rest until I can look out my window in the morning and watch the sunrise again."

Mia lets out a frustrated breath as she looks across the table at Spencer. He's watching her with pride in his eyes. He can see how much this means to her, and instead of being irritated she refuses to marry him until the case is solved, he's proud of her for taking a stand.

So am I.

"You know, I barely made it through the newspaper articles this afternoon. There were a few questions I had about the crime scene I'm hoping the case files will answer for me. They didn't keep much from the public it seems. That could work against us."

"Do you have any idea who we might be looking for yet?" Spencer asks, shifting in the booth so he's facing me. I can see the hope in his eyes, and it causes a heaviness to settle in my chest. He's relying on me. He needs me to help him break this case.

"Not yet. If I had to guess, I'd say a male, probably late twenties, early thirties. He wouldn't have to be that big to overpower Sam, especially if she was caught off guard. Or maybe she knew him and didn't fight back, which would explain why there was no sign of a struggle and the lack of DNA evidence. The rain would have washed away anything on her body but not under her nails."

"What about the rope?" Jay's voice dreamily asks. Or maybe I'm just imagining it being dreamy because there is nothing about rope that should get my motor running. Yet I feel the stir of desire hit me like a sack of potatoes.

The deep timber of his voice paired with the depth of his stare always had me tied up in knots. It appears it still does.

"What rope?" I reply. "The papers didn't mention anything about her being tied up."

At least they kept that little fact to themselves. I was starting to think the chief handed over the file to a local journalist and let them print whatever details they wanted.

"There were a few key facts that weren't released to the public. Did you look at the crime scene photos?" This from Spencer, whose knee is now bouncing up and down nervously.

"Not yet."

"Her feet and hands were bound behind her body and

then tied together. Her mouth was covered in duct tape. The teal tips of her hair were cut off." Jay's words hold no emotion behind them, as if he's put up a shield to protect himself from his connection to Sam. The victim. "The main reason I was a suspect was because I worked at the hardware store and had access to the items used. Also, I'd bought a roll of duct tape the week before spring break to fix the ping pong table after Sam decided to dance on top of it."

I can't help but smile at the memory as it flashes through my mind. She was putting on quite a show. It was the last time all five of us were together. It's also a night I'll never forgive myself for. My smile immediately falls as the thought crosses my mind.

Shaking away the memories of that night, of Sam' slamming back drinks and dancing, of sneaking off after she passed out, the images are replaced with something far worse.

Images of Sam bound together.

six

As much as I enjoy seeing my friends, they're also a reminder of why I left here in the first place. Of why I didn't want to come back. Of the mistakes I made in the short time I knew them.

Every memory I made with them, Sam was a part of it.

She was the center of our circle. The sun of our universe. She's the one that brought us together.

She knew Mia from school. They were friends long before the rest of us were even in the picture. According to Sam, they were close when they were little, grew apart and ran in different circles for a little while, but found their way back to each other toward the end of high school.

Sam met Spencer on campus her freshman year in English Lit. She sat next to him the first day and the rest is history. Spence was a sophomore who had failed the class once and was hoping not to have to take it a third time. He cozied up to Sam so she would tutor him. She reluctantly agreed, and by the time the semester was over, they'd started hanging out a little bit, only as friends according to them. I've heard there's more to the story but none of them would talk about it because she introduced him to Mia and he introduced her to Jay who was Spencer's roommate at the time.

Sam says sparks flew right away between her and Jay;

Spencer says Jay wasn't interested in her. He thought she was loud and obnoxious. The exact opposite of who Jay is. Yet, she managed to weasel her way into his heart, and within a few weeks, they went on their first date. Valentine's Day.

I came into the picture two months later when I applied for a job at Riley's Pub where I met Sam. The week after we met, I was moving into my new place where I met Jay. Well, I didn't exactly meet him. I fell into his arms and in love with him in the same moment. There were sparks, an instant connection between us. Neither of us knew we were already connected, through Sam. We'd find that out a few days later.

Over the next two years, the five of us were practically inseparable. Spencer tried to hook me up with their other friends, but I always declined, making the lame excuse that I wasn't interested in dating until after I graduated. In my defense, I was busy. Between work, school and studying, I barely had time to wash my hair let alone go on a real date. If I'd met the right guy, though, I feel like I would have made time.

It's the same reason I use now when friends try and set me up.

However, the real reason has been the same this whole time.

I wanted Jay. No one else. I wanted to be with him so much I could taste the jealousy whenever he and Sam were around. A feeling that only intensified the more time that passed. Which is why I started to pull away from everyone after New Year's Eve. It was my last semester of college and I needed to focus. I couldn't hang out every weekend until the wee hours of the morning. I couldn't go on Sam's spurof-the-moment adventures during the week when Sam had a rare night off from both Riley's and the Java Bean.

Nope. I practically locked myself away in my apartment when I wasn't in class or at work. I studied my ass off and admired Jay from afar in the hopes that my feelings for him would disappear.

The opposite happened. Absence made my heart yearn for him. He was all I could think about. Any time I did catch sight of him I felt the ache in my chest. Especially since the only time I saw him was when he'd come to Riley's to see Sam.

His girlfriend.

My best friend.

I stayed away for three long months. Not that I didn't see my friends, I just made it a point to hang out with them separately. I'd see Mia when she did my hair. Sam at work or when she'd come to my place to study. We'd have girls' lunch on occasion or go shopping.

I made it a point to limit the time I spent with Spencer and Jay. I'd see them around campus and at the gym, making sure to never be left alone with Jay. If Spencer wasn't around, I 'would bolt in the opposite direction, avoiding Jay all together.

When Sam begged me to come to a party for Spencer's birthday two nights before I was leaving for spring break, I couldn't come up with an excuse quick enough to turn her down. She'd been complaining that something was going on with Jay for months. She thought he was pulling away and was afraid he was going to break up with her. She needed me there for moral support.

My heart pounded in my chest as she went into detail. I wanted to support her, to be her shoulder to cry on, but my mind kept drifting to Jay. Wondering if this was the end for them. If I was going to finally get my chance.

It wasn't until she professed her love for him that I was able to pull my head out of my ass and focus on my friend. She was in pain and she needed to be my primary concern. Not my lust for the man who was breaking her heart. Because even if he was about to break up with her, I couldn't be with him. The line in the sand had been drawn years ago and I wasn't about to risk my friendship with Sam for a chance with Jay. Especially when I was graduating in less than two months.

The first thing I noticed that night was the difference in his stance. He was clearly on edge. Agitated. Instead of being around Sam most of the night, he seemed to avoid her. When she tried to wrap her arms around him and snuggle, he found a way to wiggle out of her arms and mingle with other people. Across the room.

And his eyes were on me all night.

When Sam climbed on top of the ping pong table to dance, turning up the music to a deafening level, he only shook his head and walked out of the room. The table leg gave out as she was climbing down, Sam sliding onto her ass on the floor with a thump. Spencer was there to help her up when it should have been Jay.

Sam was right. He was distancing himself. The more he did, the more she drank. The more she drank, the less control she had over her inhibitions which lead to a fight of epic proportions in the middle of the party. Sam was yelling and Jay was attempting to calm her down, but she was beyond reasoning with. She ended up storming off to Jay's room while he brushed it off and went back to playing beer pong with Spencer after propping the table up as a temporary fix.

I went to check on Sam, giving her time to cool off first, only to find her passed out in Jay's bed. She looked angry even in her sleep. Her mouth was pursed, and her hands were clenched next to the pillow. I studied her for a few minutes, before whispering an apology to her and begging for her forgiveness. For wanting her boyfriend. For potentially being the reason he was acting differently.

"YOU DIDN'T DO ANYTHING WRONG. WHY ARE YOU APOLOGIZING *to her?*" *Jay asked as I closed his bedroom door behind me.*

"Kissing you wasn't right," I state firmly, unable to turn around and face him.

We haven't talked since New Year's Eve. I've been avoiding him at every turn so I didn't have to have this conversation with him. It happened. It wasn't going to happen again. It was hard enough to look at my best friend without crumbling under the guilt that had taken up residence in my chest.

"If memory serves me right, I kissed you, and nothing about it felt wrong."

That kiss will live on in my memory forever. The way his lips caressed mine. How gentle yet demanding he was as his tongue traced the seam of my mouth, begging for entrance. The spark that ignited as our tongues danced, hands roaming. The way he tugged my hair to gain access to the sweet spot on my neck as he pulled me closer.

It was an amazing kiss. But it was wrong. Sam was asleep, having passed out before we rang in the new year. Mia and Spencer had left to be alone at their new place. The rest of our friends were either making out in a corner of Jay's apartment or had already fallen asleep from the copious amounts of alcohol we'd consumed since the party started earlier that evening.

We were essentially alone. No one was paying us any attention as we stood in the hall separating the kitchen from the living room.

Before the party started, I had decided my resolution would be to let go of my feelings for Jay, and instead, we ended up making out. Betraying Sam.

"I can't do that to her again, Jay. She's my best friend. If she ever found out it would destroy her."

"Tell me you don't feel something for me, that you've never felt anything for me, and I'll walk away. But don't lie to me or yourself. There's been something between us since the moment you fell into my arms." *Those same strong arms wrap around my waist and pull me tight against his chest, my back to his front.*

"Admitting it doesn't make it right."

"I miss you, Drea," *he confesses, leaning close to my ear so only I can hear what he's saying.* "I miss seeing you every day. I miss the way you bite your lower lip when you're nervous and the way your eyes light up when you're silently observing people as if you just figured out a secret you can't wait to share. I miss the smell of your hair ... vanilla and gummy bears."

"Gummy bears? My hair smells like gummy bears?" *I turn to look over my shoulder at him but stop myself before we can make eye contact. I know better. His stare makes me weak. This close up, I'll give in to him without a second thought.*

"You eat them constantly. Maybe your hair doesn't smell like them, but I can't look at a bag at the gas station without thinking about you. I have seven bags hidden in my desk right now."

All I can do is shake my head, focusing my attention back on his closed door. The door that separates us from his sleeping girlfriend.

"I have to go, Jay," *I say, attempting to step out of his embrace, but he only holds me tighter.*

"Let me walk you home."

"It's across the parking lot. I'll be fine."

"Please," he begs. "I want five minutes with you alone."

Alone. With the way my heart is hammering against my chest, begging to be freed, that's not a good idea. It's downright dangerous.

Still, I nod my head. When we make it back downstairs, the party has died down. There are a few people lingering in the kitchen watching a game of beer pong. Mia is straddling Spencer on the couch, their lips fused together. Her red hair is shielding his face from view.

Jay takes advantage of the situation, grabbing my hand, and pulls me out the door. When I try to pull away, he laces our fingers together and keeps walking, picking up the pace the closer we get to my apartment. Stealing my keys when I remove them from my pocket, Jay unlocks my door and ushers me inside. I hear the click of the door as he presses his body against mine, grabbing my ass and lifting me.

My back hits the wall at the same moment his lips find mine.

"We can't." My words are muffled as he continues his assault on my mouth, his tongue entering my mouth as I speak. Not that I'm attempting to stop him. After a few minutes, his kisses slow, moving from my lips down my chin and neck before traveling back up again.

"Five minutes," he whispers in my ear, giving it a light tug with his teeth.

"And then?" I counter, knowing nothing can change between us. Not in five minutes or five hours. The only way things could be different is if I'd met him first. If Sam and I weren't friends.

"And then we eat gummy bears and talk."

I don't have a chance to reply before his hands are in my hair, pulling my lips to his again.

Five minutes. I allow myself to enjoy every second. The feel of his body against mine. The ache between my legs that intensi-

fies with every passing second. The way his tongue sweeps over my lips, causing a shiver of pleasure to course through my body.

And when those five minutes were over, we started the clock again. And again. And again. Until we found ourselves laying on top of my bed, both of us shirtless, Jay between my legs, pressing his hard length against the most sensitive part of my body. Me, meeting his thrusts, wishing there was nothing separating us. Nothing stopping us from—

That's when my brain started firing again.

What am I doing? This is wrong. *I was about to betray my best friend in the most unforgivable way. I'd never be able to look myself in the mirror again.*

When I push Jay away, he must see what I'm thinking in the depths of my stare because he slowly backs away. Without a word, he finds his discarded shirt on the floor, pulls it back over his head, runs his fingers through his hair, and leaves without another word.

———

Shaking away the memory, I pick up the case file I abandoned before dinner. When I flip it open, Sam's dead eyes are staring back at me. She's hogtied, her mouth covered in thick, silver tape, and a large gash over her left eye.

Guilt slams into me fast and hard.

If I hadn't betrayed her, maybe Jay would have come back to town earlier. Perhaps he would have never left. He would have been there to give her a ride. She wouldn't have been walking through the park that night. She would still be here with us.

Closing my eyes, I let out a sigh.

It's not Jay's fault. It's mine.

I should have made my flight that morning. I should have been more responsible and not drank away my feelings the night before. Knowing I was going to have to face Sam when I got back was overwhelming. After dinner with my parents, I went back to my room and started taking shots. The mini fridge was stocked with little bottles of alcohol, all of which I emptied before passing out.

My parents didn't think to check on me before they headed to the airport. We were on different flights. They had no reason to think I wasn't going to make mine. I'd always been a responsible child.

Not that day. The maid found me lying on the floor of my room when she came in to clean hours after I was supposed to check out. I was mortified and hungover. After packing and rushing to the airport, I sent Sam a text asking her to cover my shift, explaining that I missed my flight.

She didn't question me about why. She agreed and told me to fly safe. Said she was excited to see me. Wanted to know what time I was going to be back in town.

Sam was a true friend. She cared about others. Would have given the shirt off her back if it meant helping someone in need.

And me? I was the bitch who betrayed her. Who made out with her boyfriend. Twice.

I'm the reason she's dead.

I may not have been the one that killed her that night, but it was because of me the opportunity was there. I'm just as guilty as the one who took her life.

seven

IT'S ALMOST MIDNIGHT BEFORE I FORCE MYSELF TO TAKE A break from reading through the case files. I'm no closer to completing my profile than when I started. The level of violence is heart-breaking. What Sam went through brings tears to my eyes. I still have unanswered questions.

Was she scared?

Did she try and call out for help?

Those are questions I'll never have the answer to. The only person who can give us the answer is gone.

There is one lingering question that I've circled in my notebook multiple times though.

Did she know her attacker?

My gut tells me she did. That she had no reason to be alarmed and that's why she had no defensive wounds. I'm certain it was a man based on the angle and depth of the blunt force trauma to her head. That's how he disarmed her. He caught her off guard and knocked her unconscious before he tied her up.

Her cause of death? Blood loss.

Had she been able to scream she might still be here.

I'm piecing together a preliminary timeline of the events when I hear shuffling outside of my door again. The only light in the room is from the lamp on the desk I'm working at. I see a shadow come to a stop in front of my door, and then disappear again … only to return a few minutes later.

I'm already shaken up after reading the case files. I didn't sleep last night because someone was outside of my door. It's time to find out who it is and put a stop to the quiet torture.

Looking around for something to protect me, I spy a tall, gold candlestick holder. After gently removing the candle and setting it on top of my open notebook, I take a deep breath and stand.

I tiptoe over to the door, place my hand on the knob, and turn as slowly as possible so as not to make a sound. When I hear the shuffling again, I pull the door open quickly and prepare to defend myself.

"Jay." There's no hiding the surprise in my voice. He's the last person I expected to find standing outside of my door.

Not that I'm disappointed. Hell, my inner cheerleader is jumping for joy at the mere sight of him. For the first time since he walked back into my life, I'm allowing myself to get a good look at him.

He's dressed in the same dark T-shirt and jeans he had on earlier. This close up, I can see how mature and defined his features have become. His jaw is stronger than I remember, more sculpted. The hint of scruff that I didn't notice at dinner has me wanting to reach out and take his face in my hands, just to know how it would feel against my skin.

It's his eyes that capture me, though. His hazel eyes are darker, the blue around the iris' lost in their depth. The way he's looking at me causing my stomach to flutter, the butterflies beginning to take flight. He holds my stare without saying a word. The intensity overwhelms me, forcing me to finally break eye contact and focus on his lips instead.

Bad idea.

"So, you are still awake." There's a hint of a smile on his lips he's trying to suppress. When I look up at him, I find him staring at the candlestick I still have raised over my head. It causes his dimple to make an appearance, the deep groove making his attractive face even more beautiful.

Slowly lowering it, I take a step back so he can come in. "Still working on the profile."

"How's that going?" he asks, walking over to the desk, his eyes scanning the photos that are scattered everywhere.

"Slowly. Why are you here?" My feet will me to move toward him, but I stay planted by the open door as he continues to study my work.

He doesn't answer me right away, the tension in the room building. It gives me time to take him in, his back facing me. He's in need of a haircut, the hair around the nape of his neck curling randomly. His shoulders seem broader as they taper down to his narrow waist. And just below that, his mouth-watering ass. The perfect accessory to the rest of his body. I can only imagine how tight it is beneath his jeans. They fit him like a glove, accentuating the perfect heart shape.

My attention is still fixated on his ass when I notice him begin to turn. Flicking my eyes away, I focus on the wall behind him. As soon as he speaks, his deep, sensual voice grabs my attention.

"You think she knew him," he says as our eyes meet.

"It's a strong possibility."

"Why?" Raising an eyebrow in curiosity, Jay crosses his

arms over his chest, causing his shirt to stretch to accommodate his large frame, and leans back against the desk.

"Gut feeling, I guess. You and I both know Sam used to walk through the park on her way home all the time. If we knew that, so did other people. Not to mention no one heard her scream, and she was less than five hundred feet from the nearest house. She wouldn't have screamed if she felt safe walking with someone."

"Your theory solidifies your timeline. If she knew him, he could have made her feel comfortable and then taken her down with the hit to her head. After that, he would have covered her mouth and tied her up. What I don't understand is why. If she was already knocked out, why tie her up? Why cover her mouth? What was the point?" Turning back toward the desk, Jay seems to be searching for something in particular.

The words are out of my mouth before I can sensor myself. "He was probably going to rape her."

Jay's shoulders tense as he reaches to pick up my notepad. "Why didn't he?"

"I don't know yet. Maybe because she wasn't alert. Perhaps he wasn't given the chance. I want to listen to all the interviews. If they talked to him, I'm hoping his voice will give something away."

Jay nods as he reads through my notes before setting them back on the desk and turning to face me again. Our eyes lock, and I suddenly feel like the shy college student I was the first time I met him, unable to speak. I feel everything, though. He's communicating with me, and what I'm reading in his gaze has my heart pounding faster, louder, begging to be freed. To be held by the one man who has the ability to heal the broken pieces.

"Why are you really here, Jay?" I finally ask, forcing my

eyes to remain locked on his as I channel any ounce of inner strength I can muster.

"I wanted to talk." The way his voice drops, I know he's not referring to the case. "We never did get to have that conversation you promised me."

"What conversation?" I ask, breaking eye contact when my voice begins to shake as I pretend to not remember the last night we were alone together. The way his body felt pressed against mine. The guilt that haunted me in the minutes, days, and weeks that followed.

It takes Jay three long strides to reach me. He stops directly in front of me, places his finger under my chin, and tilts it up until I'm staring directly into his eyes as he pushes the door closed with his other hand.

"Things have changed, Drea." His voice is filled with purpose but also desire.

"I know that." I barely manage to squeak out the words.

"Do you want to know what hasn't changed?"

It's a trick question. Don't answer it.

"No." Clearing my throat, I straighten my shoulders, focus on the dimple on his left cheek, and try to ignore the longing in my heart. "Everything has changed, Jay. Sam died and a part of me died along with her."

"Why are you shaking then? Why are you breathing like you just ran two miles on the treadmill? Why can't you look me in the eyes when you lie to me?"

Jay's right hand cups my cheek, and I involuntarily lean into it, my eyes falling closed. Warm. His skin is always so warm. Or maybe it's because he lights a fire inside of me and has since the moment I met him.

"It's always been you. Since the very first day." His words are barely above a whisper even though we're alone.

Even though we're standing closer than we have in years. Closer than we should be.

"You were with Sam. We couldn't be together."

"And now?"

Opening my eyes, I muster all the strength I have left in my body to fight my attraction to him. "Now we're celebrating her life. We're here to remember the person she was, the person we both loved. To find closure so we can move on with our lives."

Taking a step back, Jay stares down at me, his six-foot-two frame making me feel small even though I'm taller than most girls at five-foot-six.

"Do you remember the night after we met each other?" He closes the distance between us again, and I match his movement, stepping back. "I came into the bar to pick up Sam after work."

"Yeah. I offered her a ride, but she said you insisted on picking her up. She was so excited to introduce us." The look of excitement when Sam spotted Jay across the room is something I'll never forget. She waved her fuzzy pen over her head at him. When I turned to see who she was waving at, my stomach dropped.

"I was going to break up with her that night. I'd spent two days thinking about you. Looking for you everywhere. Watching out my front window for your Jeep ..." His voice trails off as he closes his eyes and sidesteps me, taking a seat on the edge of the bed.

"What stopped you?"

"I saw you. I saw the expression on Sam's face. Her only real friend was Mia and Mia had Spencer. I couldn't take you from her because I knew if I did, the chances you and I would get together were slim. If I hurt Sam, you wouldn't run into my waiting arms the way I wanted you to. You'd run the other way. You 'would be there to comfort Sam."

"You're right. I wouldn't have. The moment I found out you were dating Sam my heart sank. I also vowed not to break her heart by betraying her, no matter how much I wanted you. The way I felt stopped mattering the moment you walked into the bar that night. Sam and I had only just met, but I knew we would be friends forever. She was the happiest person I'd ever met, and I couldn't destroy her spirit. That's not what friends do, no matter how long they've known each other."

"But we did. Betray her. More than once."

His words cut deep. A reminder of the only bad thing I've ever done in my life. A reminder that I need to be strong in his presence because even though Sam's gone, he belonged to her and she deserves my loyalty in death since I couldn't give it to her in life.

"We can't change what happened, what we did. I'm glad she never found out. It would have broken her heart. That doesn't make it okay. It doesn't make it any less unforgivable." Turning my head as I speak so he can't see the devastation on my face, I stare at the discarded candle on the desk, focusing on the burnt wick. Its blackness stands out against the cream color of the wax.

Jay quickly pushes himself off the bed, 'his hands on my hips before I can protest. I'm staring at his sculpted chest, the fabric of his T-shirt barely accommodating his muscles. I wouldn't be surprised if it ripped in half from the tiniest tug of my hands.

All I'd have to do is reach up and grab his collar. Stretch the fabric to its breaking point, and with one ripping motion, his chest would be bare to me. I could trace the outline of every muscle with my fingertips. Or better yet, with my tongue. Find out exactly what he's hiding under the cheap cotton.

Does he have more tattoos?

Is he as sculpted as I imagine he is?

"Drea," Jay whispers softly as he leans in, his breath mingling with mine. "I want to kiss you. I need to know there's still something between us. There's no one standing in our way except us."

And the memories of my dead best friend. His dead girlfriend.

"It's too late," I state firmly.

"Too late for what?"

"For us. For this. Too much time has passed. There are too many things weighing on me still."

"The guilt doesn't go away, Drea. It never will. I feel it, too. I'm choosing to find happiness to drown out the guilt. To move on with my life because you never know how long you have. If there's anything we can learn from Sam's death, let it be that. Life is short. Live it to its fullest while you can. She was a free spirit. She lived. She would want you to do the same, no matter who you choose to be with."

Jay places his finger beneath my chin again and raises my head until I'm getting lost in his gorgeous hazel eyes. The blue around his irises' glimmers in the dull light of the lamp.

I want to tell him yes. I want to choose him. I want to see if there's still something more between us.

More than anything, I want him to kiss me to prove there *is* still something there.

There's no denying I can feel it. My heart wants him. It always has. As much as I tried to ignore the nagging feelings of lust, they never went away. Never dulled. Even when I'd see him kiss Sam. Or when she 'would show up at my apartment, freshly ravished.

My heart still yearned for him. To be with him. To claim him as mine.

After five years, I was hoping that feeling would have subsided. Seeing him again has done the exact opposite. The feelings I spent years pushing away, hiding from, have been rejuvenated. My heart feels like it's beating again for the first time since I left here.

All because of him.

The one man I want but still won't allow myself to have.

No amount of time will be enough to erase the guilt for the way I feel. About him. About what happened.

The guilt over the part I played in Sam's death.

The guilt over wanting Jay. Over kissing him.

Of not telling Sam the truth. Lying to her every time she asked me what was wrong. Why I didn't want to hang out. Why I wouldn't give guys a chance.

I wasn't a good friend to Sam. I was the worst kind of person. A liar and a cheat.

She deserved so much better in a best friend. She deserved someone who had her best interest at heart, the way she had theirs. Someone who cared about her feelings more than their own.

I wasn't that person when she was alive, but I can be that person now. I can put aside the longing and focus on finding justice for the wrongs that have been committed.

Instead of answering Jay, my lips part and nothing comes out.

He searches my eyes for the answer I can't put into words. The truth. My confession. Whatever he sees causes him to release my chin and slowly back away, letting himself out without a word.

Just like the last time he walked away from me.

And my reaction to his departure is identical. My tears flow freely as I stare at the door he just closed behind him. Silently begging Sam for forgiveness that I don't deserve. Praying that my love for her will at some point outweigh the love I've been carrying around for him.

eight

AFTER CRYING MYSELF TO SLEEP, I DREAMT OF SAM. OF THE first time we met. Her bright, welcoming smile. The crazy pen she gave me to use when I couldn't find one in my purse. How she made serving drinks seem more like fun than work.

Of the night she helped me unpack my apartment. The bottle of cheap, red wine we shared. Her studying every book as she put them on the shelf. Reading the descriptions on the back and asking me if any of them were worth reading. If I believed in true love because I read romance novels.

Her laughing at the idea while I contemplated telling her about my encounter that afternoon. How I was beginning to believe in love at first sight. The way it felt like my heart gave itself to someone else without asking for permission. Biting my tongue when she made fun of my favorite novel, saying the storyline wasn't believable.

No one falls in love that quick.

My dream is a mash-up of all the moments we shared before I met Jay.

She talked about him a lot in the few weeks we knew each other. It almost felt like I knew him before we were introduced.

Maybe that's why the guilt was so consuming. Because I

knew she was in love with him even though she was afraid to admit it to herself. Because I saw the stars in her eyes when she'd say his name. Because I wanted what she had.

Before I knew who he was.

Before I knew it was the guy who' saved me from falling on my face.

I wanted what she had with my mystery guy.

And then my mystery guy turned out to be her boyfriend. The guy who brought her mother flowers when he picked Sam up for their first date. The same guy who was always giving her funky pens for work because he said the fuzzy tops reminded him of her colorful hair. The guy who sent her cute texts while she was at work saying he missed her, wanting to know if she needed a ride home so she didn't have to walk.

Jay was a gentleman. He showered Sam with affection. Was always buying her little gifts and bringing them to her at work. He drove her around whenever her car broke down and never once complained.

He was perfect.

He was also hers.

I never told Sam about my mystery guy. I had intended to but when she arrived that night to help me unpack, she was in a foul mood. It had been a rough night at work. One of the locals in town had been harassing her all night, hitting on her even though she flat out told him she had a boyfriend. We drank wine, and I let her make fun of my romance novels and bitch while we unpacked until we both passed out from a mixture of exhaustion and too much alcohol.

Not that I forgot about him after that day. Nope. Jay's timing just happened to be as perfect as he was. He showed up to pick her up the next night as I launched into my story. I was just to the part in the story where I tripped when he walked in. My story was long forgotten as I watched her run across the now empty bar and launch herself into his arms.

His eyes were on me.

Mine on him.

And I knew in that moment that I could never have him. I wouldn't do that to Sam because I'd be devastated if someone did that to me. Love at first sight or not. It didn't matter that I had already given him a piece of my heart.

Hoes before bros.

Sam was my hoe.

That sounds horrible. Referring to her as a hoe, especially since she's gone now.

Shaking away the memories as I climb out of bed, I head into the bathroom and turn the shower on. I'm getting an early start today so I can work on the profile. My alarm went off at six o'clock, but I've been laying in bed, snuggled under the covers for the last thirty minutes.

Once steam begins to billow out from behind the curtain, I slip out of my yoga pants and pull my tank top over my head, folding both and putting them in my suitcase. I'm about to step out of my underwear when there's a knock at my door.

I freeze, my underwear resting just below my butt cheeks.

Who the hell is knocking on my door this early in the morning and why?

Another knock.

I can't very well ignore it.

Pulling my underwear back on, I let out a sigh as I walk over and answer the door after a third set of knocks sound.

"Yeah?" I ask, raising my voice so they can hear me

through the older wooden door. Judging by the age of the B&B and the historic feel to the decor, the door is more than likely solid wood.

"I come bearing gifts," I hear Jay say as the handle begins to turn.

"Wait!" I scream and dart for the bathroom, slamming the door behind me.

"Did I catch you at a bad time?" His voice is muffled by the bathroom door as I hear him moving around the room.

Cracking the door open and peeking my head out, the strong aroma of coffee hits me. "Java Bean?" I ask when he looks in my direction.

"Are you naked?" His voice is low, almost a growl as he stares at me. The only parts of my body that are visible are my head and my shoulder, my hair falling in long waves, cascading over my shoulder as I use the door to shield the rest of my nakedness.

"I'm about to get in the shower. Why are you bringing me coffee so early? Don't you like sleep?" My attempt to change the subject fails as his eyes bore into me from across the room.

"Are. You. Naked?"

"Of course I'm naked. I don't shower in my clothes." He takes a step toward the bathroom, but I stop him with the shake of my head. "Don't. I'll be out in a few minutes."

"I've waited for you for seven years, Drea. I can wait a few more minutes." His eyes never leave mine as he steps back, setting the tray of coffee on the table next to the bed.

"Oh yeah?" I laugh. "And what? I'm just going to throw myself at you after I shower? That doesn't happen in real life, Jay."

"No, but I'm guessing you didn't bring any clothes in there with you since you weren't expecting company."

Shit.

Glaring at Jay for a long second before shutting and locking the bathroom door, I pull my hair into a tight bun on top of my head and step under the scalding spray. I'm still cursing him under my breath as I shut the water off and wrap a towel around my body.

True to his word, Jay is waiting for me when I walk back into the room. He looks relaxed sitting up on the bed with his back to the headboard. He's staring down at his phone but looks up when I clear my throat.

"Gorgeous," he states, tossing his phone aside and sliding off the bed.

"Stay where you are." Holding out my hand in a stop motion, Jay stays seated on the edge of the bed while I stare him down. "I don't remember you being this dangerous."

"Tempting," he counters.

"What?"

"I think you meant to say tempting. And yes, you do remember me being this tempting. In fact, I remember one incident in particular where I'm pretty sure you were caught drooling."

Rolling my eyes at the memory, I don't bother to reply. Instead, I grab clean clothes, careful to keep my towel wrapped around me as tight as possible, and head back into the still steamy bathroom to dress before I fall for Jay's charm and throw myself at him. The idea has crossed my mind no less than a dozen times since I heard his voice on the other side of the door.

Especially after I got a good look at him. Dark wash jeans and a black button-down shirt with the sleeves rolled up to his elbows. He was fresh out of the shower, his hair still damp. The stubble that had graced his handsome face last night was gone.

Jay's relaxing on my bed again when I emerge fully dressed and ready for the day. Black slacks. Black and white pinstriped blouse that dips low into a V. The same outfit I wore to my grandmother's funeral last year.

Jay doesn't seem disappointed in what he sees. There's a smirk on his face that is attempting to melt my heart and almost does when his damn dimple makes an appearance. I keep my stance strong under his gaze, even when I feel the moisture beginning to pool in my panties.

"Ready?" he asks.

"For what?"

There are a few things I'm ready for. None of them are appropriate to share out loud. All of them would cause more problems. Only one would bring me temporary joy and relief. It wouldn't last, though. The feeling would fade, and the guilt would creep back in.

"I brought breakfast so we could work on the profile. I figured I would offer my services since I know the case about as well as anyone except Spencer."

Breakfast. *That I can handle, right? It's just food.*

"Maybe I should ask Spence for help then." Crossing my arms over my chest, I don't miss the way his eyes flick to my low neckline before quickly returning to my face.

"His vision is clouded by now. He's seen those files a thousand times. It's been a few years since I've looked at them until last night."

"How does a guy who loves computers and studies IT end up going to the police academy by the way?" I inquire, images of disassembled computers scattered around Jay's bedroom filling my memory. He was always tinkering with something. Taking it apart and putting it back together. Making it faster, better than it was before.

"The rug was pulled out from beneath him when he

graduated. His temper flared when he's questioned for the murder of his girlfriend. But the final straw was when no one would give him any answers. I stayed, you know. For months. I was here, waiting for them to find whoever killed Sam. When they couldn't, and Spencer decided to join the academy, I followed."

I can hear the frustration and anger in his voice. Even if I couldn't, the way he's clenching his fists would have been a clear indication of how infuriating of a time it was for him. I can't imagine what he went through.

Everyone stayed but me. I ran from this place as if my life depended on it. The farther I ran, the less my heart ached. The intense pressure in my chest lifted, but it was only temporary. Not even a week after I returned home, I fell apart completely. I was alone and empty. The one person I wanted to call, the one person who would be able to talk me through the tough time, was the one person I couldn't.

"And now?" I ask. I need to stay focused on the conversation or the past will overwhelm me. I'll be right back to the person I was when I left here last time. Lost and alone.

"Now I work for the government."

"Care to elaborate?" My body begins to move toward him as if it's being pulled by an invisible rope. Scratch that. A magnet. I've always thought Jay was magnetic. The pull he has on me feels charged.

"Not at the moment. Look, I want to try and help you. If nothing else, I'll be your sounding board," he offers, handing me a cup of coffee.

"That's not exactly how I work things out but I'm guessing you have no intention of going anywhere." Raising my eyebrow at him in question as I take a sip of my coffee, I don't miss the slight shake of his head.

"Not until it's time for the memorial brunch."

Agreeing with a nod, I gather up all the files and we spread out on the bed, working in silence for a little while. It's almost time for us to leave when Jay starts frantically searching through everything.

"What are you doing?"

"The crime scene pictures. Where did you put them?"

Looking at the piles of pictures and papers around me, I finally spot the photos he's talking about and hand them to him.

"This," he says, tapping the photo with his finger. "This is what we're missing."

Leaning in and looking over his shoulder, I search the photo for any clue as to what Jay is referring to.

"I don't see anything."

"That's exactly the point. No footprints. It was rainy the night she was murdered. That's part of the reason there wasn't any DNA. We're also positive he wore gloves. But footprints don't wash away. Sam was in the grass. There should have been some breaks in the grass. A fresh indent."

"It's not like you can erase footprints," I point out.

Raising my eyebrow at Jay, he explains his theory. We already know Sam was attacked on the sidewalk. There was blood spatter found on the concrete. Her attacker then carried her into a secluded area of the park surrounded by shrubs where he tied her up and left her to die. He would have had to walk through a small, grassy area off the path to dump Sam's body where he had, just out of sight.

Jay thinks he walked all around the area to flatten the grass so his footprints wouldn't have been visible to the naked eye. And with Sam in his arms, the extra weigh would have made it easy for him to walk across the grass light enough on his way out.

"It's a good theory," I compliment Jay. "So, it's someone who's strong enough to carry Sam a decent distance, and also carry a bag with the rope and tape in it."

"Did you notice the rope wasn't cut?" he asks, pointing at a different photo.

Taking the picture off the top of the pile, I study the rope for a few minutes, focusing on the ends, before setting it back down. The ends appear sealed with glue. There are no fraying marks.

"So, he bought the length he needed." It comes out sounding like a statement instead of a question. I have no idea where he's going with this theory, but I want him to get there faster. We're running out of time.

"Which is hard to do. Apollo Hardware only sold one length of this kind of rope back then. Nylon rope is used for anchoring boats. The rope we sold was matched to the depth of the deepest lake in the area. This one is not nearly that long, which means—"

"He bought the rope somewhere else," I interrupt, grabbing the list of people interviewed.

"Exactly."

"So, are we looking for someone from town who was aware of this or a visitor?" My fingers quickly scan down the list of individuals who were initially interviewed.

"I think your' initial profile is correct. It's someone from here. Someone who knew Sam and her habits. That was a path she traveled all the time. I feel like someone was watching and waiting to strike. Think about it. Most of the town is asleep at that time of night. The only people awake are the college students, and most of us were still gone for spring break."

Staring at Jay, my mind starts running a million miles an hour. Clues are starting to piece themselves together.

"We can only eliminate three people from the list if you want to focus on people from town. That leaves us with close to two dozen people as potential suspects. We need to narrow the list down."

"We should listen to the interviews," he suggests as the alarm on my phone goes off. Reaching over, he silences it and then adds, "After the memorial bunch."

I realize he's found a way to secure more alone time with me but that doesn't stop me from agreeing. I feel like we're onto something. That the answers are in front of us, we just have to look a little deeper.

Sam's murder has always felt like a puzzle someone dumped out of the box onto the table, pieces flying everywhere, and we couldn't put it together. Now, it feels like the puzzle isn't scattered everywhere anymore. We have all the outside pieces connected. We just need to work on the little details and soon we'll have a finished picture of what happened.

More importantly, of who is responsible.

We have hope.

nine

Jay and I walk into the memorial lunch together still discussing the case, oblivious to those around us. That is, until Summer steps in our path. My voice and feet both falter instantly.

The mere sight of my old life flashes before my eyes, memories flooding my brain. The first time I met Summer. I gave Sam a ride home after work and she invited me in. Summer was still awake, sitting at the kitchen table, laptop open, drinking a cup of coffee. It was after midnight, and I remember thinking I wouldn't be able to fall asleep if I were to have caffeine this late at night.

She immediately closed her computer and gave us her full attention. There was a genuinely happy smile on her face. We ended up sitting around talking for hours. Summer wanted to know everything about me. Where I was from. What I was studying in school. If I liked working at Riley's.

And when I left, she pulled me in for a hug that warmed my heart. It was the moment I realized I'd been invited as part of their family. She adopted me as her second child that night. Treated me as one of her own from then on. Would get on my case if she thought I was working too much and not enjoying life. I was invited to every family meal, every holiday, and there were presents for me under their tree at Christmas time.

For the first time in my life, I felt like I was part of a family. My parents gave me the material things I needed in life, but Summer and Sam provided my emotional needs. They showed me love in a way I didn't realize I was missing.

"Summer," Jay greets her warmly, pulling her in for a hug that she returns with enthusiasm.

"It's so nice to see you again, Jay. How was your drive?"

Summer and Jay make small talk while I zone out. I take in my surroundings, the people standing in little groups conversing. All here to celebrate Sam. To remember her. To celebrate her life.

For me, it's shining a bright light on what happened to her more than anything. Sure, there are things I've forgotten that are coming back to me. Moments we shared. Memories we made. However, I can't help but focus on the real reason we're all here.

She was killed.

Summer's voice cuts through the haze, highlighting my very thoughts.

"Are you two helping with Sam's case?" she asks.

Jay's back stiffens. "Something like that," he replies, not wanting to give her false hope.

We decided on the walk over that it would be best to keep everything to ourselves for now. Any conclusions we draw. Any details we piece together. We don't want anyone to get excited, and we certainly don't want the person responsible to get wind of our efforts and flee town.

The more we talked, the more certain I became that it's someone from Great Falls. The fact both scares me senseless, because he's still out there, and sad because we could have prevented it had we paid better attention to those around us. To the people in our own community.

"Care to enlighten me?" she continues when Jay offers nothing more, looking between the two of us.

"As soon as we know more, you'll be the first person I call," I promise her, pulling her into my side to avoid eye contact.

The three of us take our seats at a table in the corner. The university has gone all out decorating the lobby of the student center in remembrance of Sam. Bouquets of pink and teal balloons are spaced around the large area. Pink and white flowers in teal vases adorn each table covered in a white tablecloth. But the centerpiece of the event is the large buffet running along the front windows judging by the crowd of people lining up to dig in.

As soon as Spencer and Mia arrive, the five of us get in line to fill our plates. I try not to think about the fact that we're basically at a memorial service. That the black outfits everyone is wearing symbolizes death. Or that we're only gathered because of a tragedy.

It feels like we're at her funeral all over again. Not that I remember that day. I have flashbacks from time to time of Mia forcing me in the shower, curling my hair, and helping me into my black dress. The service itself is a blur, and most of the luncheon after as well.

The one thing that stands out from that day is the way the four of us—me, Mia, Spence, and Jay—stood united. We sat together. Held hands. The guys carried Sam's casket while Mia and I consoled a devastated Summer.

And here we are again. The four of us, along with Summer, gathering because of Sam. Because some asshole decided to take her life for a reason we have yet to figure out. Of all the emotions I'm feeling right now, anger is the most prevalent.

Still, I keep my head held high and force myself to smile and laugh at Spencer's jokes. I put on my brave face and push away the sadness and loss that's clutching my heart, making it hard to breathe, let alone eat. The same feeling that's had a vice grip on me since setting foot back in this tiny town I once called home.

A microphone comes to life as I'm about to take a bite of my potato salad, the light puffs of a tapping sound bouncing off the high ceilings. It silences the voices around us to a low hush.

"Hello, hello," the dean says. Spinning in my seat, I find him standing behind a podium on the far side of the room. "Thank you all for being here today. Sam was a bright light in our community, and although taken far too soon, made a lasting impact on many of us. One such person is here today to share with you his memories of Sam. If you would please join me in welcoming Jay Ross," the Dean concludes, waving his hand in our direction.

My mouth drops open in shock as Jay stands from his seat next to me and makes his way to the podium while the small crowd claps. After shaking the dean's hand, he takes the microphone from him and casually rests against the side of the podium.

Jesus. He looks absolutely stunning. The artwork on his left arm stands out against his shirt and draws my attention momentarily. My eyes travel north, landing on his eyes. I couldn't help but notice how his shirt brought out the colors earlier, brightening the soft gray.

It's a damn good thing he's not giving a Ted talk right now. Not a single woman in this room would retain any information.

Jay Ross is sex on a stick.

"Hello. First, I'd like to thank the university for giving me the opportunity to be here today to share with all of you the love I had for Sam. I'd also like to thank Summer, Sam's mom, for allowing me to date her daughter and for welcoming me into their family with arms wide open."

I glance over my shoulder to see Summer blow Jay a kiss and place her hand over her heart. I wasn't the only person she adopted. We were all one big family, Mia and Spencer included.

"I'm not going to lie and say my relationship with Sam was perfect. We all knew her, so we knew how stubborn she could be." Laughter rumbles through the crowd but I can't tear my eyes away from Jay. "She was a feisty little thing. Always full of energy. Ready for her next adventure. She found a way to make everyone smile, even in their darkest times. She brought out the best in those around her. And when she loved, she loved with all her heart.

"I wasn't good enough for Sam. I didn't deserve her. I knew it, and I tried to push her away in the beginning, but she wasn't having it. She just pestered me until I agreed to take her out and the rest is history. Our first date was a bit of a disaster. It was Valentine's Day, and I didn't make a reservation. We spent most of the night driving around, looking for somewhere to eat. We ended up in an Arby's parking lot three towns over. It wasn't my finest moment, but by the end of the night, she had me hooked. Life was an adventure to Sam. That night was no different. It didn't matter that we were eating curly fries in a dimly lit parking lot. We were together, talking, getting to know each other, and that's all she wanted from our first date. The food and location didn't matter. We were together and that's what was important to her. From that moment on I tried my best to make her as happy as she made me, but I feel like I failed a little more every day. If she were here, she'd probably disagree with me. She 'would try to fight me on my statements. And you know what, I'd be okay with that. Because that would mean she was here still. I'd fight with her every day for the rest of my life if given the chance."

Jay breaks eye contact with the crowd, lowering his head and taking a deep breath. Once he raises it again, his composure is back, and his eyes are locked on mine.

"We all have memories with Sam that we'll hold onto for the rest of our life, that we'll keep close to our heart, so we don't forget her. Remember the good times, forget the bad. Remember her smile and her laugh. The way she brightened up a room when she walked in. Lock those details away, and when you think of Sam, think of her fondly. That's what I'll always do. She will always have a place in my heart. Thank you."

He doesn't break eye contact with me as he places the microphone on the podium and makes his way back over to our table. Turning back to face our friends, I scan their faces to find tears in their eyes, Jay's words striking deep.

"That was a beautiful tribute," Summer says, reaching across the table to take Jay's hands in hers after he's seated again.

"She was a beautiful woman with a big heart," he replies, placing his free hand on my leg beneath the table.

I'm still staring at their clasped hands when the dean commands the microphone again, startling me. Blinking twice, I feel the first tear fall. Before I can wipe it away, Jay's taken my face in his hands and his thumbs catch the strays, and the set that follows after.

"Thank you all again for coming out. We'll be releasing lanterns in honor of Sam tonight at dusk from the fifty-yard line of the football field. Please make sure you're at the stadium no later than six o'clock so you have time to personalize your lanterns. Tonight's speaker as we send our love to Sam up in the heavens will be her best friend, Andrea Morris." The mention of my name has me closing my eyes, releasing a fresh set of unshed tears. "Tomorrow will also be a day of celebration. The first annual Samantha Bridges Memorial Race will begin in the parking lot of Riley's Pub at nine o'clock and conclude at the unveiling of the new fountain at the center of Central Park where the fountain will be dedicated in Sam's honor. I hope you can join us in celebrating Sam's life as we mourn her death as a community on the fifth anniversary of her tragic passing."

With that, I hear the microphone turn off, the speakers popping softly overhead. When I finally open my eyes a few minutes later, Jay and I are alone at the table. He's still holding my face in his hands and staring at me with concern etched between his brows.

"I'm okay," I say, letting out a sigh, my voice lacking the conviction I was hoping it would have. There really is no point in lying to him. Everyone is riding the same emotional rollercoaster I'm on. The feeling of loss is a freshly opened wound again. I'm not in this alone, yet I feel the need to push him away. Push them all away.

"You need to get some sleep." He's studying my face as he speaks.

"Well, if someone wasn't knocking on my door at all hours of the night, maybe I would be able to," I counter, raising my left eyebrow at him in challenge.

"I promise I won't tonight." His words are a complete contradiction to the growing smirk on his face. Before I can question him further, he's pulling me out of my seat, lacing our fingers together, and we're walking out the door. I barely have time to wave at Mia and Spencer who are talking with Summer and the dean. All four of them are staring at us as we glide out the exit. Mia's eyes are glued on our clasped hands, a sinister smirk on her face.

"Where are we going?" I ask as I almost trip over my feet in an attempt to keep up with his long strides.

"You're tired."

"And we're rushing back to my room because you want me to take a nap? We have to listen to those interviews, Jay. Time is not on my side here. The chief expects me to deliver the profile in forty-eight hours. I can't stop to rest right now. I need to nail down de—"

"We," he interrupts. "We need to nail down details. You're not doing this alone."

"Fine. We need to eliminate potential suspects. Go over the files again to make sure we didn't miss something important that could help us identify who did this to her. I can sleep when I'm dea—"

I cut myself off as Jay jerks me to a stop.

"When I get back home," I quickly correct myself.

"I lost you before, Drea. I don't plan on letting that happen for a second time. You need to rest. You're running yourself into the ground trying to solve this case. It's not good for you. You'll think better after a nap."

"You never lost me," I protest, averting my eyes, but that does nothing to cool the heat creeping up my neck from his stare.

You can't lose what you never had, I think to myself.

Releasing my hand, Jay slides his arm around my waist and tugs my body to his. Leaning in close, he nibbles my earlobe before whispering words that crack the last of my resolve.

I want him. Damn the consequences.

I'm not strong enough to resist the magnetic pull he's had on me the last seven years. Not anymore. I fought the good fight for as long as I could. Now, I'm giving in. Willingly. I'm going to allow myself to have the one thing I've denied myself.

Jay.

He's not a piece of bread. It's not like you've been avoiding carbs all these years. He's a person. There's a reason you kept your distance. Ignored your heart. Her name is Sam.

Shaking my head in an attempt to shoo away the negative thoughts of my conscience, I take in our surroundings. We're standing in the middle of the sidewalk. Campus is practically deserted with the exception of the attendees of the brunch, most of whom are still mingling in the student center. Still, I make sure no one is watching us. The last thing I want is an audience.

"I lost you the night Sam introduced us." His words are punctuated with a kiss to the sensitive spot behind my ear. "I lost you after I kissed you on New Year's Eve." Another kiss and I'm starting to tremble in his arms. "I lost you the night I tried to claim you before spring break." He moves lower, kissing his way down to my collarbone, eliciting a moan. "I thought I lost you for good when Sam died."

Then he kisses me again, this time tugging the collar of my shirt to the side so he can kiss my shoulder, and a shiver runs up my spine, causing goosebumps to pebble my skin. My heart is pounding, my breathing strangled. All the heat in my body has rushed to my lower extremities, my need multiplying rapidly.

"I won't lose you again. You can try and fight me all you want but I know you still want me as much as I still want you. Since the day we met. I felt it then and I feel it now. I see it in your eyes, in the way your body responds to me.

The way it's always responded to me. From the goose-bumps that cover your skin to the way you claw at me like you can't get close enough. How you kiss me like your life depends on it."

My body has a mind of its own. One hand is gripping his shoulder, the other his waist. I've slid my left leg between both of his, and even as he speaks and presses his lips against my skin, I find myself leaning in.

"What do you want?" I ask, breathless, my words coming out sounding needy.

"You, Drea. I want you. That's all I've ever wanted." He kisses his way up the side of my neck, and my eyes flutter closed the closer he gets to the place I want them most. When he pulls away, his lips never touching mine, I open my eyes to see exactly why.

The usually light depths of his hazel eyes are dark, completely masking the dark blue hues around his irises. His pupils are dilated. There's a wild look in his eyes to match the uneven breaths he's taking.

"We have to go," he says as voices in the distance grow louder.

As soon as I nod, he takes my hand again and we're rushing back to the Hideaway. To my room. Where we'll be hidden from prying eyes. Alone. With no one to stop us but ourselves.

ten

THE LATCH OF THE DOOR ECHOES THROUGH THE ROOM AS I stare straight ahead. I feel Jay approach rather than hear him. The hairs on the back of my neck are standing on end before he steps up behind me, wrapping his arms around my waist. My eyes drift to the mess we left on the bed, photos and paperwork covering the blanket everywhere except where we had been sitting.

"I'd like to have that conversation now," Jay says, his lips pressing against the side of my neck. Tilting my head to give him better access, I let out a little hum as a reply. "I even brought snacks."

I hear the rustle of cellophane, and then feel something pressed into my hand. When I look down, there's a mini pack of gummy bears in my palm.

"My favorite."

"I know. I still buy packs when I go to the gas station."

"You hate gummy bears," I state, turning in his arms so I can look into his eyes. Hazel globes I've wanted to get lost in since the moment we met.

"Yes, but there's this girl who loves them and I've been holding out hope that one day I'd be able to share my stash with her."

His eyes are alive as he takes in every aspect of my face, raising his hand to trace the path his eyes take. From my right cheek to my ear and then my chin. He gives me a little pinch before rubbing the pad of his thumb over my bottom lip, parting them as my tongue licks the seam.

Without asking this time, he leans in and gently presses his lips to mine for a brief moment. When he pulls back, he seems to contemplate his next move before leaning back in, this time stealing my breath.

My arms wrap around his neck, pulling him closer, begging him to deepen the kiss, as my fingers tangle with the hairs at the base of his neck. Needing no more urging, Jay's tongue dives into my mouth, and the dance begins.

Our breath mingles.

Bodies pressing against one another.

I'm lifted off the floor, my back hitting the wall as my legs wrap around him, drawing him closer.

The second his hard length presses against my core I let out a moan that's captured by Jay and silenced by his kiss. His hands grip my ass so tight I'm sure he's going to leave marks. I return his enthusiasm, tugging his hair so hard I wouldn't be surprised if I ripped some out of his head.

That doesn't stop his assault on me or mine on him.

He leans back only long enough to remove his shirt, pulling it over his head without unbuttoning it, and tossing it across the room. His lips return to mine, demanding control of the kiss. It's not until my hands begin wandering over the hard ridges of his chest that he lowers me to the floor and takes a step back.

We're both breathing heavily. The gleam in his eyes is primal. I recognize the look. It's the way I feel deep in my soul. It's filled with need, pent up for years and ready to finally be released.

"Shirt," he demands.

Without giving it a second thought, I raise my arms

over my head, and seconds later my shirt goes flying in the same direction Jay's did. His eyes devour every inch of my bare skin, heating me despite the cool temperature in the room that has my skin pebbling with goosebumps.

"You are so beautiful, Andrea," he says, reaching out and tracing a path from my neck to my belly button with just his finger. "Inside and out, you are the most gorgeous woman I have ever met."

If my panties weren't already drenched from his kiss, his words would have done it.

"I've been waiting for this moment for so long. I've wanted you every second of every day I've known you. I may have been with another woman, but it was you I wanted. Then and now. Forever. Always."

"Then have me," I hear myself say.

That's all the encouragement he needs to pull my body against his and reclaim my mouth. This time he's slow, gentle. Savoring every moment as he explores my body with his hands, caressing parts of me that haven't felt attention in far too long.

When I feel the button on my pants release, I suck in a breath and my body stills.

Yes, this is what I want. What I've always wanted. To be with Jay.

Why am I nervous now?

Oh, yeah.

I haven't been with a man in exactly a year, the last time being on the anniversary of Sam's death. My assistant convinced me to go out for drinks, and I let a guy who reminded me of Jay take me home that night. He was clumsy and smelled of stale beer and cigarettes.

Still, I pictured Jay when he touched me. Held my breath and imagined it was Jay when he was inside of me. I kept my eyes closed and lived in a fantasy land until he collapsed on top of me two minutes later.

As soon as he fell asleep, I left. He called me at least a dozen times in the following days. Sent me flowers at the office and sweet text messages before finally giving up. I couldn't even bring myself to let him down easy. I ignored him until he went away.

He wasn't Jay. He never would be. There was no reason to pretend. It would only cause us both pain in the end, and I was living with enough as it was.

"Don't worry," he pushes the band of my pants over my hips and releases them to pool at my feet, "I'll go slow."

"I don't know if I can handle slow," I hear myself confess.

I'm already on edge, ready to explode. I felt what he was packing when he had me against the door. I'm going to come undone from anticipation the second he pushes inside of me.

"Thank God." He lets out an exasperated sigh as he begins fumbling with his own pants, his lips still pressed against mine. "I'm not going to last much longer."

As soon as his pants are shed, left in only his boxer briefs, Jay begins carefully but quickly picking up the mess we left on the bed. Once everything is stacked neatly on the desk, he extends his hand to me, and I place mine in his. The second our fingers connect, he pulls my body to his and captures my lips again.

The fire inside of me sparks and roars back to life as if it's been an hour instead of a minute since I felt his touch.

He walks us backwards toward the bed, and once we reach it, he gently lays me down on top of the blanket, crawling over me to cover my body with his. We stay like this for a while, our kisses heating up and then slowing down, hands wandering, exploring, bodies rubbing against each other.

Jay rolls so I'm on top of him, straddling his waist. The second I'm seated on top of him, I grind my hips and watch his eyes roll to the back of his head as he lets out a long growl.

"You can't do that again unless you're ready for us to lose the rest of our clothes. I won't survive."

My only response is to grind against him again, this time slower. Once. Twice. The third time, his hands fly to my hips. Gripping and guiding my body as I continue to grind against him.

I can feel my body reacting to his. I was already close, and every time I slide forward, I get closer. My body is strung so tight it's going to break at any moment. Shatter into a million pieces.

"Best torture ever," Jay whispers beneath me. His eyes are closed but he's still helping me rock my body up and down his.

"Jay." His name comes out as a plea. I need him. I need more.

A devious smirk grows as he lifts his hips, pressing into my core as I grind against him again. His dimple is winking at me as he does it again. Once more, this time as he opens his eyes, and I fall apart on top of him, my body slumping forward as little orgasmic aftershocks rip through me.

Jay doesn't stop his torturous assault. He flips us over, spreads my legs, and presses his impressive length against my core again and again until he finds his own release moments later.

The only sounds in the room are from the ticking clock

on the wall and our labored breathing as we lay side by side, attempting to catch our breath.

Staring up at the ceiling, I count to ten and then back to one, breathing in and out slowly. My heart is pounding so hard against my ribcage it feels like it's attempting to escape. And I know exactly where it would go.

To find the man I've been trying to forget the last five years.

The one man who's owned my heart since I first met him.

Jay takes my hand in his and laces our fingers together. We lay in silence as our bodies come down from the high. I'm afraid to speak, to ruin the moment we just shared. Worried we've crossed a line we can't jump back over.

You don't want to jump back over that line. This is what you've always wanted.

My damn subconscious is right. Again. I like being on this side of the line. It's where I've dreamt of being. In Jay's arms. In his life. In his heart.

One of those things has happened now. The other two are still to be determined. We have a couple of long, emotional days to get through. Days that will constantly remind us of the past. Of the person we both loved. The reason we couldn't be together.

Had I moved into my apartment earlier …

Had he not given in to her charm so easily …

Had she never met Spencer …

There are a million what-if scenarios I could throw at the universe, but they don't matter one bit. The simple truth is that I was late to the party. She met him first.

"Stop," I hear Jay state firmly, the bed dipping as he turns toward me, propping himself up on his elbow so he peer into my eyes.

"I wasn't doing anything," I reply, guilt laced in my every word.

He couldn't possibly know what I was thinking, could he?

"This isn't about anybody but us. Two grown adults. People who care about each other very much. I don't give a shit what anyone else thinks. All I care about is you. This moment. The way you looked when you completely let go. Knowing I did that. Your lips were parted, your eyes closed, head thrown back, and you were pressing against me. Your body begging for more."

Running the back of his hand over my cheek, down my neck, and continuing until he's gripping my hip, Jay pauses to relish my body, but not for long.

"Live in that moment, Drea. Don't let the guilt from the past dictate your present. Don't let it stop you from having what you want. What you've always wanted. From being with me. Because I want to see that expression on your face again. A lot more. Very soon."

Pressing my elbows into the mattress, I force my body up and seal my lips against his. The hand that was resting on my hip is now holding my head hostage as Jay devours my lips. His body rolls on top of me, and a familiar sensation begins to build as he rocks his body against mine.

Soon must mean now. His recovery time is impressive.

"Too. Many. Clothes," he says between kisses as he works his way down my neck.

"Yes." The single word comes out as a hiss as he nips the sweet spot where my neck and shoulder meet.

Jay's hand slides up my back, and I raise off the bed as far as I can so he can unclasp my bra. Once I feel the fabric release it's hold, I start pulling it away from my body. Sitting up, Jay steadies my hands and slowly removes my bra, taking in the sight before him with great admiration.

I've always been ashamed of how large my breasts are. They're more than a handful and the last thing I would describe them as is perky. My areolas are large, and I have a mole above my right breast.

"Perfection," he states, his eyes never leaving my chest. My nipples pucker as the cold air brushes across them. He seems to notice and bends to take one in his mouth and the other in his hand, my back arching off the bed in response as I hold his head captive against my chest.

"So responsive," he coos, moving to pay the other nipple the same attention. I don't bother to reply with anything more than a moan when he bites down on the sensitive bud.

While his mouth and left hand work their magic on my breasts, his right hand takes a slow and torturous adventure down my side, across my stomach, and slips beneath the thin material of my thong, gently tugging as I wiggle with anticipation.

Once I'm free of the binding undergarment and the only thing between Jay and I are his boxer briefs, I wrap my legs around his waist and pull him tightly against me. A growl escapes him as his movements become frenzied. Shimming out of the last of his remaining clothes, I attempt to help with my toes only to be met with resistance.

"If I take them off, there's no going back," he murmurs against my chest before lifting his eyes to mine.

Our eyes remain locked as he slides out of his underwear, repositions himself, and runs his shaft against my slick center. When I let out a huff of air in frustration, he drives into me in one quick thrust until he's fully seated and I'm moaning loud enough the entire B&B knows what we're doing.

Jay lays motionless inside of me.

"Please," I beg.

"Please, what?" he teases, his mouth reclaiming my breast.

"I need you to move." My plea comes out strangled as I attempt to press up against him, only I'm not strong enough to lift his body off mine. He has me pinned to the mattress, trapped in a state of sexual frustration.

"Like this?" he asks, slowly retreating slightly.

"Mmmhmm," I moan. "More."

Jay finds a slow, lazy rhythm, pistoning in and out of me, working my body into a frenzy.

"Drea," he moans as he picks up the pace slightly. "I don't know how much longer I can last. You feel so good. I'm close."

The need dripping from every word causes me to clench around him, my impending orgasm looming closer.

"Me." Huff. Moan. "Too."

"Come for me, baby. Let go. Let me hear you," he urges, lifting his head from my breast as he drives himself deeper. "Open your eyes for me, Drea. I want to watch you fall apart beneath me."

That's all it takes. My eyes fly open as I arch my body against his, my orgasm shattering around him.

"You're so fucking beautiful," he praises, his words spoken so softly I can barely hear him over the pounding of my heart as another orgasm begins to bloom.

Pushing himself up, Jay reaches beneath my ass and lifts me, his already impressive length going even deeper as he continues to drive into me.

"Again," he demands. "I want one more."

"I can't," I lie as my inner walls clench, making him feel that much larger.

"You can. We can. Together."

"Harder," I hear myself demand. Two deep, punishing thrusts and I'm coming again, Jay's release following mine within seconds.

My body is exhausted. My heart pounding but content.

It's my mind that refuses to leave me alone.

As soon as Jay pulls out of me, the only thing I can think is that I slept with Sam's boyfriend. That I've betrayed her in a way that I'll never forgive myself for. It doesn't matter she's no longer here. That she's been gone for five years. That I did my best to stay away.

I took what I wanted, and he wasn't mine to take. He'll always belong to Sam.

"Are you okay?" I hear Jay ask as he wipes away the tears I didn't even realize were falling.

"I don't know." It's a lie, but how can I tell him the truth? That I'm lying naked next to him, regretting what just happened while feeling completely content at the same time. I'm a hot mess and my emotions are all over the place.

"Tell me what's wrong and we'll find a way to make it right, Drea. I promise."

"You will always be Sam's and we've dishonored her memory." My honesty catches me off guard.

Jay frowns at my confession as he wipes away another set of stray tears. "Sam and I had a complicated relationship. She wanted more than I was willing to give her from the start. I think she knew I was in love with someone else, but she wasn't ready to let me go. She wasn't ready to move on. She fought hard to make our relationship work even when it became obvious that it couldn't.

"So, I slowly pulled away, hoping she would break up with me. I was a coward. I shouldn't have let it go on as long as it did. I shouldn't have been afraid to break up with her, but I was. The last thing I wanted to do was hurt Sam because I did care about her. She was my friend before anything, and I wanted to remain that way."

"But you led her on for years, Jay. Years." I'm yelling at him even though his face isn't even a foot from mine.

"I know, and I'm not proud of it. I'd go back and change things if I could. Perhaps she would still be here if I'd manned up and called it quits. Maybe she would have found someone else that made her happy and he would have picked her up from work that night. What I know for sure, though, is that no matter when we broke up or who made the decision, you wouldn't have given me a chance back then. You would have stuck by Sam's side no matter what.

"There are no sides anymore, Drea. You aren't stuck in the middle. You're not being pulled in two different directions. It's just me and you. Two people who have cared for each other for a long time and deserve a chance to see where this life can take them. Together. To find out if the feelings they've harbored for years are real."

Swallowing the lump in my throat, I reach up and caress Jay's face.

I want his words to be true. For us to be able to entertain the idea of being together. Without guilt nagging at me. I don't think it's possible, but right now, as he rolls his body on top of mine and presses his lips to the side of my neck, I want to make it my reality. I want to try. I want to let go of the past and open my eyes to the possibility of a future with the only man who's ever held a piece of my heart.

eleven

THE NAP I DESPERATELY NEEDED WAS A FORGOTTEN thought. Instead, Jay and I spent the afternoon exploring each other's bodies. Getting to know each other intimately.

Multiple times.

On the bed.

In the chair.

Bent over the desk.

And finally, in the shower while we washed each other from head to toe. The room smelled of sex when we left, our bodies still humming, but our sins had been washed away.

For now.

Sins of the past and present.

My exhaustion started to set in as we arrived at the lantern release, twenty minutes late, as everyone was gathering on the football field. The sun was just starting to kiss the horizon, fields of orange, yellow, and red illuminated above the forest of trees that ran along the western edge of campus.

The dean is waiting for us, a forced smile on his face as we approach, two microphones in hand. He immediately hands me one, and I take it without hesitation, setting my lantern on the ground at my feet.

"The ceremony starts in five minutes. I'll be introducing

you, Andrea, and then the lanterns will be released one by one as you speak."

Nodding my head in understanding, my eyes follow his line of sight to the growing crowd in front of us. There are at least fifty people here already and more still walking into the stadium. Most are faces I recognize from town or old classmates. Mia and Spencer are standing off to the side, waving us over.

When I lift my hand to return their gesture, forgetting Jay's fingers are laced with mine, it looks more like I'm punching the air in celebration. Mia's smile brightens while Spencer remains stoic, his face unreadable from this distance.

"You should go and stand with them," I urge Jay, attempting to pull my hand from his. He's not giving up without a fight though. The same way he refused to let go on the walk over here when we passed my old boss from Riley's Pub.

"We'll see them later. I'd rather be here for you in case you need me."

"What makes you think I need you?" I retort, unable to hide my smile at his gesture.

"If you would rather do this alone ..." he starts, taking a step toward where our friends are still watching us with interest.

I pull him back as I hear the dean begin his introduction, and Jay wraps his arm around my waist, pulling me in front of him. Resting my head against his broad chest, I close my eyes until I hear my name.

Sliding the button up on the microphone, I stare at the little green light signaling that it's on.

I can do this.

After sucking in a deep breath and letting it out slowly,

I bring the microphone to my lips and close my eyes again. If I can't see them, I won't know if they're looking at me.

"Sam was more than just my best friend. She was like a sister to me. My other half. The yin to my yang. Where she was outgoing and spunky, I was quiet and reserved. She dressed to stand out while I used my clothes as a way to blend into the crowd. Her hair ... gosh, she loved to get creative. A different color every month, sometimes more often than that. Her favorite colors were pink and teal. In her mind, they were bright enough to stand out against her boring brown strands. They brought color to her pale skin. And let's not forget her signature red lipstick. I'm pretty sure I never saw her without it."

Pausing, I take another deep breath and open my eyes. Jay tightens his hold, reassuring me without saying a word that I can do this. His presence alone has calmed me.

"Sam and I met at Riley's. She made a hell of a first impression. She was bold and a tad bit crazy, but she was damn good at what she did. She loved her job and found a way to have fun in a stressful environment. She didn't take shit from anyone but could dish it out. After the first night I worked with her I knew we would always be friends. There was something about her that spoke to a part of me that was missing. She brought out parts of my personality I didn't realize existed."

Stopping to watch a few of the lanterns release, I snuggle deeper into Jay's arms before continuing.

"For two years we were practically inseparable. I have more memories that I can count. From funny stories to boring nights spent studying together. Day trips shopping for her next outrageous outfit. Countless parties I barely remember. And we still hold the beer pong team championship."

I feel the rumble in Jay's chest as Spencer's burst of laugher echoes across the open field. I knew he'd get a kick out of that comment. After all, we stole the title from him and Jay.

"The last time I talked to Sam was the day I left for spring break. I had invited her to come with me, but she didn't want to spend the money on a lavish trip. She was saving for a new car, one that didn't break down every other day. She was close to her goal, and we had planned on going car shopping when I got back. That didn't happen. Someone stole that dream from her. Stole all her dreams from her.

"The same person ripped out a piece of my heart that day. I lost my best friend. Summer lost her only daughter. Sam was only one person, but she touched each and every one here. We all still feel her loss, even five years later because when she was killed this town lost its innocence. A town I had always seen as safe. A place that prided itself on the community that lived here. And one of their own destroyed everything Great Falls stood for."

Realizing the accusation I just made, I wait for people to start turning around and staring at me in shock. No one moves, all eyes are lifted to the sky as lanterns continue to be released. Floating to heaven. To Sam. With messages of love on them. For her and only her. From the people whose lives she touched in her short time on this Earth.

"As the last lantern flies tonight, close your eyes and focus on your favorite memory of Sam. Something that made you laugh. A time when she made you feel special or brought a smile to your face. That's the kind of person she was and that's the way we should remember her. Saying good-bye is never easy but that's what we're doing tonight. Sending Sam off with love in our hearts and holding on to the memories we made with her. Together, we are healing our broken souls."

Turning the microphone off, I drop it to the ground and bend to retrieve my lantern, Jay releasing his hold on me for the first time since arriving. I immediately feel the loss, my heart aching for him to pull me close again.

When did I become so clingy?

As soon as Jay's lantern is lit and flying skyward, he turns to light mine, but I shake my head. Looking to the crowd, I wait until the last lantern is released. When the fire in mine is burning brightly, I give it a nudge toward the heavens and say a silent prayer.

I promise I will find who did this to you if it's the last thing I do. We won't stop until we have answers, and someone is held accountable. I love you, Sam. I always have and I always will.

Blinking, I feel the first tear fall as I finish my prayer.

Please forgive my heart for loving him. I never meant to hurt you, in life or in death.

My tears continue to fall as I watch the lights of the lanterns illuminate the night sky, the sun having fallen beyond the horizon now. They drift higher and higher until they're out of sight. All except one. One that's lingering lower than the rest.

Mine.

Of course.

Please forgive me, I beg Sam, clasping my hands together over my mouth as I speak.

As if Sam was listening, a light breeze rustles my hair, and my lantern disappears from sight.

"Thank you all again for coming tonight. We hope you'll join us bright and early for the race and stick around for the dedication afterwards." The dean's voice carries across the open field as people start to make their way back toward the parking lot.

Mia and Spencer head in our direction, navigating their way through the crowd, as Jay leans down and whispers in my ear.

"Are we telling people or is this our little secret?" Running the back of his hand down my arm, his fingers tease mine.

"Are we telling them what? That we screwed each other's brains out? I don't think that would be appropriate, do you?"

A deep rumble bursts from Jay's chest as Spencer and Mia reach us. Spencer looks between us, his head bobbing back and forth, waiting for one of us to explain what's so funny.

"So …" Mia starts, staring at me expectantly.

"I need a drink," I state firmly, stepping away from my circle of friends and falling in with the last of the crowd.

"Riley's?" Mia asks, sliding up next to me and linking our arms.

"Unless there's a new bar in town," I retort.

Riley's was always busy because there was only one watering hole in a town this size. If you wanted to go out and let loose, Riley's was your destination of choice. Unless you wanted to deal with neighboring townies. Not that there was bad blood, we just knew to stick to our own city limits.

Plus, we walked to Riley's so we didn't do something stupid like get wasted and try and drive home later. My apartment was fifteen minutes straight down Main Street. So if I didn't work Monday nights, I'd go in for three-dollar margaritas. Or if I wasn't scheduled on a random

Friday night, you would find me being pulled up on stage to sing karaoke by Sam.

Thursday's were my favorite's though. It was college night. We sold mixed drinks by the pitcher and wasted college students tipped better than anyone. We limited them to two pitchers of their drink of choice and then cut them off. Their bills were no more than twelve dollars and they'd hand you a twenty and tell you to keep the change. Multiply that by forty college students each and it made for happy waitresses.

"Nope," Mia replies, popping the p for emphasis. "You know nothing ever changes around here."

We walk in silence across campus and toward the local watering hole. Spence and Jay are a few paces behind us, deep in hushed conversation. Every time I look over my shoulder to make sure they're still following us, Jay's eyes meet mine and his smile grows. As if to say, *I'm not going anywhere. Don't worry.*

The second I step across the threshold, my eyes falling immediately to the dirty concrete beneath my feet, memories assault me. If Jay hadn't been behind me, I may have fallen on my ass from the force I felt pressed against my chest.

My heartbeat increases the farther we make our way into the bar. A clear image of Sam leaning over the bar, her ass in the air as her feet dangled above the ground flashes through my mind. My twenty-second birthday, the week after school started. All my friends singing to me over the country music playing in the background as Sam brought out a piece of peanut butter cheesecake, my favorite, with as many candles as the little piece could handle sticking out of it.

Seventeen was the magic number. She claimed she

counted eighteen but I'm fairly certain one fell off at some point.

Sliding onto the last stool at the end of the bar, a sensation tickles my spine, causing goosebumps to pebble my skin and the hairs on the back of my neck to stand on end.

I was sitting in the creeper's seat.

The guy that would come in every night as we were about to close. At least a decade older than us with wire-rimmed glasses and dirty brown hair, there was nothing special about him. Nothing that made him stand out in a crowd. Except maybe the fact he hit on every waitress that came within earshot of him.

He thought he was God's gift. Apparently, he was popular in high school. A track star, I think. Everyone knew him. Everyone loved him. His parents owned the Royal Theater, but when his father fell ill, he took over the business. Every day, after the last showing of the night, he would stop in for one beer and leave.

He always gave me a bad vibe. There was something off about him, about the way his eyes seemed to track you around the room.

A familiar poof of black hair teased high on top of her head fills my vision as I blink away the memories. Mindi's hands are fisted at her hips and she's glaring at me with a mixture of love and hatred in her eyes.

"Hey, Mindi," I greet her, quickly sliding off the stool and moving to step behind the bar to give her a hug.

She welcomes me with open arms but not before giving me a tongue lashing that would make any mother proud. Because that's what she was. A mother hen to all of us back then. She'd kick our asses when we needed it and was our shoulder to cry on when our hearts were heavy.

I came to her after Sam died. We grieved together.

Cried over a bottle of whiskey. Toasted Sam and the memories we made with her.

Mindi blamed herself for not working that night. For not being there to watch over her.

I blamed myself for not making it home in time to work my shift. For Sam being in the wrong place at the wrong time.

The Jack Daniels helped us drown our sorrows. Once Jack left us, we sought comfort in his friend, Jim Beam.

"You've been gone five years and you think you can walk back into my bar—"

Not her bar though she's worked here longer than anyone else and the owners barely bother to show up when she's here, knowing she'll take care of everything.

"—ask for a hug and pretend you didn't even bother to say good-bye to me before skipping town? I have news for you, Andi, that's not how we do things here in Great Falls. Or have you forgotten?"

All I can do is smile. I missed her. More than I realized. More than I want to admit to myself. *I've missed all of them*, I think as I make eye contact with each of my friends as they attempt to hold in their laughter.

When I lock eyes with Jay, my breath hitches and my knees threaten to give out. It's the same look he gave me this afternoon before we began tarnishing every surface in my room.

"I'm sorry," I whisper, unable to pull my eyes away from Jay's.

"You don't sound sorry. You sound like you're about to come in your panties," she hollers. Well, that's one way to get me to pay attention. "Stop staring at Jay like you're a horny college student and give me a damn hug."

I can feel all eyes on me as Mindi and I embrace. People

are calling her name, demanding drinks, but she ignores them. When she finally releases me, I hurry back around to my seat and avoid eye contact with all my friends.

"So," Mia starts, leaning in close, "does someone need to go to confession, or should I just draw my own conclusion based on the blush in your cheeks?"

So much for keeping what happened between us private. It makes me wonder how I was able to keep my feelings for Jay a secret all those years. Or if I really was?

twelve

WE STARTED WITH SHOTS OF JACK, SAM'S FAVORITE. AFTER three in quick succession, I challenged the guys to a game of pool. Jay raised his eyebrow at me, silently questioning my request, but didn't back down. I knew he wouldn't. Neither would Spence. They've never been able to resist a challenge.

The thing is ... I'm horrible at pool. I miss the easiest shots. Put the cue ball in the pocket more than any other ball. And constantly forget if I'm stripes or solids, especially after I've been drinking.

But there is a glimmer of hope on my side. Mia is a pool shark, and the guys know it. She'll have to carry the team if we're going to have any chance at beating the guys.

"Who wants to make a little side wager?" Spencer asks as he arranges the balls in the little triangle thingy.

I'm not surprised by his question. Spencer likes to bet on almost everything. Beer pong. Pool. How to spell words. He's willing to wager money on the littlest things because he likes to be right.

"Dude, I already lost fifty bucks to you before I got to town. I'm out." Jay holds his hands up in the air and backs away from the table slowly, almost bumping into a frenzied waitress as she darts behind him with a tray of drinks.

"You shouldn't bet against me if you don't want to lose,"

Spence quips, removing the triangle and spinning it between his fingertips.

"You tricked me."

"No. I hadn't gotten an answer yet. How is that tricking you?"

"You knew if you bugged the hell out of her, she'd finally relent. I told you as much."

"You shouldn't have taken the bet then." Spencer shrugs his shoulder and smiles at Jay, taunting him.

Stepping between the two of them, I place one hand on each chest and they both fall silent. "Why do I have the feeling you two were betting on me?"

"Because they were," Mia whispers in my ear as she breezes past me, smacking Spence on the back of the head before snagging the cue ball and heading to the other end of the table to break.

"Seriously?" I ask, looking between the two of them.

"He said I couldn't get you to come. You know I never back down from a challenge."

"And what's your excuse?" I ask, my question directed at Jay.

"I knew if I challenged him he would find a way to convince you to come." Jay's smile widens as he reaches for my waist, pulling me in close. "I would have called you myself if I thought it could have made a difference."

"And if I hadn't come?"

"If I remember right," he begins, his lips grazing the shell of my ear, "you came multiple times."

Wiggling out of his embrace, I smack him on the chest and walk to the opposite side of the pool table. Mia sends the cue ball sailing down the table. It smacks into the solid green ball in front, sending the rest scattering but nothing drops.

"What's it going to be, ladies?" Spencer asks, leaning over the table and lining up his first shot. "Wanna put a little money down on the game or are you scared to lose like my partner is?"

Spencer pulls the stick back and very gently knocks the cue ball forward into the solid blue ball, sending it into the side pocket with ease. I don't remember him being that good at pool.

"I'll take that bet," Mia finally replies as he lines up his next shot. "Best two out of three. Lord knows you only perform good once a night."

The meaning behind her words catches him off guard, causing him to send the cue ball the wrong direction, knocking in our yellow stripe. Mia giggles behind her hand as Spencer glares.

"You did that on purpose," he accuses, handing his stick off to Jay as he rounds the table, marching in our direction. Mia hands me her stick and pushes me away.

"Your turn, California beauty queen," Jay says loud enough to draw Spencer's attention away from Mia before they start arguing.

Spencer stops dead in his tracks, his head whipping around as he screams at Jay, "Mine! That's my nickname for her."

"Calm down, Romeo. We all know that," I say, pointing the stick across the table at him.

All three of my friends are staring at me in shock as I refuse to break eye contact with Spencer, left brow raised. He's waiting for me to back down and it's not going to happen. That's when I realize I defended Jay, something I have never done before. Not because he didn't deserve it, but because it wasn't my place.

It was Sam's.

If I had, it would have been obvious how I felt about him back then. Not just to Sam, but everyone. But Sam's not here anymore. And now I'm sleeping with Jay. And apparently that means I've taken up the task of defending him even though I shouldn't.

It's not like we're in a relationship.

Hell, after this weekend, I'm not even sure when the next time I'll see him will be. Until we part ways, though, I plan to fully enjoy every second I have with him. Even if we have to be clothed part of the time.

Spencer breaks first, his laugher coming out in a huff as he bends over. Jay's not far behind him, slapping Spence on the back as he howls. Mia is more reserved as she covers her mouth with her hands, the slight bounce in her chest the only indication she finds my sudden dominant personality amusing.

Rolling my eyes at all my friends, I line up a shot and quickly take it, sinking the solid purple in the corner pocket. I'm dancing in a circle, fist pumping the air, when my eyes lock with Mia's. She's shaking her head at me as she digs through her purse. Retrieving what looks like a twenty-dollar bill, she slaps it in Spencer's palm.

"I thought it was best two out of three?"

"Yeah, but we made a side bet," Mia informs me, taking the stick back and pulling me away from the table so Jay can take his shot. "I was confident you'd go at least the first game without hitting one of their balls in."

"Spencer doubted me and he won because—"

"We're stripes, hun. You sunk a solid." Mia's still laughing and shaking her head as Jay takes his shot, dropping two balls in quick succession.

Damn it!

The rest of the first game is uneventful. I miss all my

shots, Mia makes all hers, and we take the first game. Irritated at their loss, Spencer heads to the bar for a round of drinks while Jay racks. I'm forced to break at the same moment Spencer returns with four bottles of beer.

His dumb ass walks behind me as I'm drawing the stick back, and I nail him in the balls. Hard judging by the groan he made as he fell to the ground, beers tumbling down with him, splashing the back of my pants and covering most of him.

"If I knew you were going to make it so I couldn't have kids, I wouldn't have invited you this weekend," he jokes as Jay helps him up.

"Mia and I had a side bet," I retort, turning my back to him and lining up to break again.

I'm not sure where my air of confidence is coming from, but I slam the stick into the cue ball, sending it sailing down the table, directly into the ball at the top of the triangle. The sound of balls clinking against one another as they scatter around the table brings a smile to my face. I hold that smile as I turn back to face Spencer once again.

"Nice break," Jay states, his smile matching my own, the dimple on his left cheek appearing deeper.

"You bet against your partner?" Spencer asks, taking the fresh beer Mindi hands him, tipping it back before I can answer.

I look over my left shoulder to Mia for support, but she only shrugs her shoulders.

"No, but it got you to stop bitching for a second while I took my shot, didn't it?"

Spencer shakes his head, adjusts his groin, and snatches the stick Jay's extending to him. He has his game face on as he takes his next three shots, sinking two balls in a row before barely missing the last one. Mia comes back and matches his efforts. Jay impresses me by sinking three balls and then clearly missing his final shot on purpose. It doesn't slip past Spencer either who calls him out, but his empty threats don't seem to bother Jay as he sips his beer, leaning on a bar stool in the corner.

I make my first shot surprisingly but miss my next one. Movement from across the table catches my eye as I hand off the pool stick. When I look up, I find a young waitress clearly flirting with Jay though he's not even looking at her. His eyes are locked on mine, dancing with amusement.

Stomping over to where they are, I slide between Jay's open legs and steal his beer, taking a sip. The hoppy flavor hits my tongue, making me want to cringe, but I hold it in as I slowly swallow, turning my attention to the brunette with her hand on Jay's shoulder.

"I'd like a Malibu and pineapple juice please," I say, my voice as sweet as the drink I just ordered.

"Oh," she says, taking a step back and avoiding eye contact. "Sure."

I feel the rumble in Jay's chest beneath where I'm resting my hand as I watch her scurry over to the bar and ask Mindi for my order. Mindi lifts her eyes, and when they meet mine, I can see the amusement dance in hers. I have a full drink sitting on the other side of the pool table.

"Why do I feel like you just peed on me? I didn't realize you had a jealous bone in your body."

Ha! If he only knew how jealous of Sam I was every time I saw them together.

It's not something I'm proud of and I don't plan on telling him. Ever. I've lived with jealousy wrapped around my heart for years. Honestly, my response to seeing someone hit on Jay surprises me as much as it does him.

Still, if I only have a few days with him, it's going to be me touching him. Me flirting with him. Me showing him attention. Not someone else. Certainly not someone who doesn't know him or what he's been through.

"Green isn't a good color on me," I state flippantly as I attempt to turn around and watch our friends battle it out.

"I bet you'd look beautiful in anything you put on," Jay whispers in my ear, his right hand gripping my hip. "We should get going soon. We have plans tonight."

"Do these plans involve clothes?" I ask, my voice taking on a seductive tone I didn't realize I possessed.

What is happening to me? Who is this bold person taking control of my personality tonight?

"Clothing can be optional, but I guarantee I won't be able to focus on anything other than the taste of your skin if you're naked."

The thought alone causes a shiver to run up my spine. I'm fairly certain Jay's tongue possesses magical powers.

"If I have to wear clothes, I'm guessing you want to work on the profile." It's more of a statement than a question. We spent the afternoon fooling around, literally, and not working like we should have been.

What we did instead was more fun, though.

"Our time is running out." It's a simple statement but I also hear his concern laced in every word.

To build a profile.

To figure out who may have killed Sam.

To fit together the last remaining pieces of the puzzles.

Our time is running out to solve the case before it's closed.

What I really heard him say is, *"We're running out of time together."*

Mia manages to clear the table on her next turn, and

victory goes to the ladies. Jay settles the tab with Mindi while Spencer gives Mia her money back from their side bet, both leaving with the same amount they came with. I call it a win-win. However, I can see the disappointment in both their eyes.

They've always challenged each other and gone back and forth. It's always seemed natural. Right now, as we say good-bye to our friends and part ways, I can feel the tension between them. Either things aren't as perfect as they appear, or the stress of this weekend is finally getting to them.

I can't imagine what they went through every day for the last five years. Waiting for answers. Staring out your front window, a perfect view of the park where your friend was murdered. A constant reminder of what happened always in sight.

"Do you think they're okay?" I ask Jay as we cross the street, heading down State Street toward the Hideaway, my home away from home for a few more days.

"I think Spencer is stressed out, and Mia needs closure more than any of us. I think they've been living this nightmare every day for the last five years, and as much as they want to run away from it the way we did, they can't. They've put down roots here. They're building their life here."

"Why here, though? I know Mia's family is here but that's not a reason to stay. She could always come visit."

"Mia won't leave Summer."

The mention of Sam's mom brings tears to my eyes. I was like a second daughter to her. She treated me as one of her own. I spent holidays with Sam and Summer instead of flying back to California.

And I up and left her. Because I was hurting. Not giving

any thought to the fact that she not only lost her daughter, her reason for breathing, but she would also lose me. I was selfish in my escape. I thought I needed to handle how I was feeling on my own. I didn't want people to see me break.

A fresh start was all that was on my mind. Somewhere far from here. Away from the devastation I saw on everyone's faces. I couldn't handle the weight that was bearing down on me. The guilt and the sadness were overwhelming, and I believed running was my only escape from the pain.

I see now how wrong I was. The only people who will ever be able to help me heal, to help me move on, are the ones who bear the same pain I did. We all lost Sam. I wasn't the only one hurting, yet I selfishly pushed everyone away. I left them to deal with the aftermath of her death. Disappeared for years. Stopped taking calls. Ignored their attempts to contact me.

Taking a deep, cleansing breath as we walk up the porch steps of the Hideaway, I make a vow. I've already promised Sam I would find who did this to her, but I want to amend that statement.

I will find who did this to Sam but I'm not going to do it for her, or even for me, I'm going to do it for Summer. For the woman who lost both her daughters and still found a way to go on. To survive when the darkness could have easily swallowed her up.

For our friends who have spent the last five years reliving the pain of that day. Who have dedicated their life to keeping Sam's memory alive.

I'm going to find who did this for everyone who knew and loved Sam.

thirteen

As soon as we are back to my room, Jay and I laid out a timeline of the events of Sam's night that have been confirmed by the reports included in the case file.

The pub was slow, so she was sent home early since she was on overtime after picking up my shift. With all the college students on break, Sam was working extra hours. Not that she minded. She was saving her money for a car and she knew even with a slow week, the extra shifts would bring in the last little bit of cash she needed.

She left the bar at roughly ten o'clock. This was confirmed by her timecard, showing she clocked out at one minute after the hour, and again by a patron who saw her walk into the park around quarter after ten as he was getting out of his vehicle that was parked in front of Riley's.

There were four text exchanges after she clocked out. Sam sent the first one to me at ten-ten asking if I'd made it back to town yet. According to the log the police obtained from her cell provider, I replied twenty-nine minutes later.

I remember reading her text that night and replying before I walked in the door of my apartment. That means I was driving past the park around ten-thirty as I made my way home.

The second text Sam sent was at ten-twenty-one to Jay, asking if he wanted to come straight to her house when he got back to town. Jay didn't respond to her text until close to midnight saying he was still almost an hour away and was going home to bed.

There are witness statements from a couple that was making out in the park that night until it started to rain. Neither of them saw or heard anything. They entered around ten-thirty and left close to eleven o'clock, coming and going close to where Sam was attacked, using the east entrance.

Summer called the police to report Sam missing a little after eight o'clock the next morning when she didn't show up for work or answer her phone. She found Sam's bed still made, as if she hadn't slept in it the night before, so she called Jay to see if Sam was with him, but he was asleep. By the time she called me, I was already in class and I had to send her to voicemail.

Sam's body was found at eight-thirty in the morning by a neighbor as she was walking her dog. The dog started to go crazy and pulled the elderly lady into the alcove where Sam's body was hidden behind a line of bushes.

The police determined Sam died between ten-thirty and eleven o'clock at night. Her cause of death was blunt force trauma to the head which caused her to bleed out.

Her walk home from Riley's was less than a mile. It usually only took her twenty minutes, which was why she didn't mind walking when it was nice outside. She said it helped her relax. I get it. After a long shift it often took me hours to find sleep if I didn't unwind with a glass of wine or a book.

After looking at the timeline we spent most of the night piecing together, Jay and I began to speculate what may have happened between the time she sent her last text to Jay at ten-twenty-one and eleven o'clock. If she entered the park at quarter after, she would have arrived home no later than ten thirty-five, give or take a few minutes.

If she was looking at her phone, texting, she could have been caught off guard.

When I pointed out that fact, I immediately notice the change in Jay's demeanor.

She was attacked immediately following her last text on the sidewalk where blood spatter was found. The assailant then carried Sam into the alcove, covered her mouth with tape, and tied her up to keep her silent. He already had her hidden when the couple entered the park but may have reconsidered carrying out the rest of his plan when they didn't leave immediately, instead ducking out of the park at an unknown time more than likely with a plan to return later that night.

No one saw or heard anything when she was attacked.

No one saw or heard anyone on the streets that night that appeared unusual or out of place.

In fact, it was a quiet night in Great Falls with all the college students either recovering from spring break or still out of town. I don't remember seeing anyone out and about as I made my way through town.

"So, what now?" he asks, pulling his shirt over his head and tossing it on the floor near the foot of the bed.

"We know what happened, when, and how. We need to figure out the who since they're the only one who can tell us why." My words come out slowly as I take in every naked inch of his chest. Rock hard abs, defined muscles. His tattoo swirling around his shoulder blade, dipping toward his chest but stopping short.

I want to trace it with my finger. Every intricate detail. The black ink against his bronzed skin -

"What do we know about him?" Jay snaps his fingers in front of my face to get my attention. When I lift my eyes to his, he's smiling at me, reading my mind like I'm an open book.

Every dirty thought.

Ideas of what I'd like to do to him.

What I'd like him to do to me.

Focus, girl.

"You would never suspect him," I state, averting my eyes down to the list of people the police interviewed in the days following Sam's murder. "He's everyone's best friend but knows how to blend into a crowd. People know of him but don't know him. Not on a personal level. He keeps his feelings to himself. Doesn't allow people to get close to him. This is generally a sign of verbal abuse from his childhood. More than likely from a father figure, but his relationship with his mother would have been strong. She is who he compares all women to. Which is a big part of why he's often single, unable to maintain a healthy relationship for a long period of time."

Closing my eyes, I try to focus on the facts, on what I've learned over the years. On the murderers I've studied, interviewed. I've gotten in their heads. I've been able to decipher things about them they didn't even know. Why they killed. How they chose their victims. When it all started, the urges to take a life.

Most don't give it much thought. They are the way they are. They feel the need to kill so they follow through with the action. It empowers them. It's the high they're seeking. To keep them from going insane.

"He's charismatic and girls trust him easily. Instead of

bringing a girl flowers, he would go overboard and buy her jewelry in a vain attempt to impress her. To keep her. To buy her attention because at his core that's what he craves. I'm guessing he wanted Sam's attention and she turned him away. He convinced himself that he was in love with her, but she wouldn't give him the chance to show her. That would have angered him, hurt his feelings." My mind is reeling as I tuck a stray strand of hair behind my ear and take a deep breath before continuing.

Jay watches my every move intently, my skin heating beneath his stare. He's making it hard to focus. A fact he knows, and judging by the smile on his face, he's proud of the effect he has on me.

"More than likely, he had been watching her for a while. There are two main types of killers. Organized and unorganized. The man who killed Sam falls into the organized category. He planned this. He knew what he was doing. I'd classify him as a pathological, obsessive killer. That's a big part of why I think it's someone local. Sam was habitual. She always took the same path home through the park. She worked the same schedule at both the Java Bean and Riley's every week. But we were all gone on spring break. There was no chance you were picking her up and giving her a ride. No chance I was working that night. He was prepared when he attacked her, which means somehow he knew she would be there when she wouldn't have under normal circumstance."

The pieces are starting to fall into place as an image of a man with no face clouds my vision. He's dressed in black head to toe. A hood pulled over his head, blocking his face. I have to shake my head to make him go away.

"He's probably a regular at Riley's. That could be how he knows her. Something Mindi said tonight struck me as odd. She said she should have been there, watching out for Sam. She and I were the ones who used to close on Sunday nights. It was like that since I started. She had regulars that would come to visit her. It makes me wonder if it's one of them. Someone who knew Mindi wouldn't be there. He wouldn't be missed that night and he knew Sam was going to be there instead of me."

"Don't you think you're digging a little too deep into something that could be a pure coincidence?"

Grinding my teeth to keep from saying something mean and nasty, I glare at Jay for a few minutes without defending my position. This is what I do. I dig deeper. The little details often seem insignificant when they're actually the glue that holds the puzzle together. We need to figure out those details.

Once I feel I can compose myself, I take a deep breath and let it out.

"That's my job, Jay. To look at every potential aspect. To try and walk in his shoes. I will never understand why they do what they do completely, but I can attempt to see how he planned it out. Because this was premeditated. Which means he'd been planning this for a while. Which is how he was able to gather materials from out of town without drawing suspicion."

"That! That's what we need to find out who he is. The rope. We need to find out who sells rope that length."

"It's been five years, Jay. If the initial investigation had caught it, there would have been a chance to link it back to a suspect. It would have been slim even back then, though. He's smart. His moves are calculated. He would have paid cash. Bought the tape and the rope from different store in different cities on different days. He's that organized. That calculated. He would have anticipated being caught and took every precaution to avoid it."

"And he left no DNA behind," he says, frustration clear in the way he lets out a huff of air.

"He wore gloves. More than likely a hat. Dressed in dark clothing. The fact that it rained that night worked in his favor. If there had been any DNA is would have been washed away."

"Which brings us back to square one. A male, from Great Falls, who is a closet murderer that no one would ever suspect. This town is full of friendly faces. It could literally be anyone at this point."

"Actually, we're probably closer than you think. Remember, we're building a profile for the police. Yes, we have the files and all the information and that helps our profile become more complete. At the end of the day, though, all I'll be able to do is present the profile to the chief and his officers. If they can identify a potential suspect, that's great. If not, we can't do much more to hand them the person responsible. We've weeded out people who don't fit the description. We have a complete timeline of events. That will help them narrow down the suspect pool even further."

Silence descends upon us. This is the worst part of my job. Not being able to pinpoint who the suspect is by name. I know his personality. I often understand what drives him to kill. But his identity is a mystery.

Which is a big part of why I stepped away from working with active investigations and focus now on studying those that have already been caught. The criminals that have given us every detail about themselves. The pieces of the puzzle are already in front of me. I just need to fit them together so we have the entire picture and not just a snapshot.

Picking up all the files strewn around the room, Jay and I crawl in bed shortly after midnight. My mind is still reeling yet I fall asleep in minutes, his warm embrace making me feel safe after spending hours dissecting more details of Sam's murder.

When my alarm goes off a little after six o'clock, I reach for Jay, but his side of the bed is empty, the sheet still warm. Tossing back the blanket, my feet hit the cold, hardwood floor, sending a chill up my spine. Reaching for my phone, I contemplate calling him to see where he went when the door slowly creaks open and Jay slides in.

He's freshly showered, his hair still damp. Little water drops are scattered across his shoulders and the back of his T-shirt, causing the light gray to darken.

It's obvious by the way he closes the door he's unaware that I'm awake. He's turning the handle and holding it in a vain attempt to keep the latch from sounding. When it finally slides into place, the sound echoing through the room, Jay's shoulders tense as he slowly turns to face the bed.

He visibly relaxes when he sees I'm already awake. He has two cups of coffee in his left hand, this time in signature Hideaway mugs. They're deep red with the B&B's logo on the front in white and black etching.

"Raiding the coffee station without me?" I joke, standing and taking the outstretched mug from him.

"I figured you would sleep a little longer and thought coffee would be a peace offering after last night."

Last night?

"And why would you need a peace offering?" I ask,

blowing across the steaming liquid before taking a small sip.

Jay's eyes watch my lips in fascination, his tongue darting out, licking his bottom lip as I pull the mug away.

"I was a little frustrated and I didn't want you to think it was with you. This case has me wanting to pull my hair out," he explains, stepping closer, taking back my coffee and setting both mugs on the table behind me. When he grips my hips, my body seems to come alive.

Just one touch. A simple caress of the skin. That's all it takes for me to want him. To consider climbing his body like a tree and wrapping myself around him.

It's always been that way. My body has always responded to his touch which is why I used to avoid it at all costs. I couldn't hide my reaction to him, and the last thing I wanted was for Sam to notice. To see the lust in my eyes that I was harboring for her boyfriend. Or worse, the lust in his that should have been reserved for her.

I would give him a wide berth when he'd walk near me. Avoided putting myself in a room alone with him. I'd sit across the room or on the other side of Sam if necessary. Anything to avoid him brushing up against me and causing a reaction I wouldn't be able to hide.

The one thing I never could avoid was his stare, though. His eyes seemed to find mine in the crowd. Speaking to me without words. Telling me everything I wanted to hear at a time when those very words, if spoken aloud, would have been the catalyst that destroyed both of our relationships with Sam.

Those same eyes are staring into mine right now. Communicating with me in a way I feel deep in my soul. The difference between this moment and all those stolen glances of our past?

No one is here to stop us from showing each other how we feel with actions. From speaking the words that would have brought our world crashing down around us all those years ago.

After the fight I put up, resisting the pull Jay had on me, my entire life fell apart anyway. It shattered into pieces with one phone call.

fourteen

THE SIGNIFICANCE OF TODAY WASN'T LOST TO ME WHEN JAY cupped the back of my neck and pulled my lips to his. The intensity behind his kiss didn't erase the years of betrayal I've held onto. It didn't ease the guilt I still carried in my heart.

Those things only dulled while a different feeling blossomed.

Waiting. Wanting. Longing. Feelings I buried down deep over the years.

Afraid to admit them to anyone. To say the words out loud.

Yet, I've called his name in my sleep. On multiple occasions.

The first year I was back in LA I would dream about him almost nightly. That we were given our chance to be together. His kisses always stole my breath, and I would wake up panting, the ache between my legs too much to bear. I'd be forced to take care of myself. And every time I would start to teeter on the edge of the cliff, Sam's laughter would ring in my ears and I'd start crying.

The worst was when I had company.

I compared every date I went on with what I thought it would be like if the guy across the table were Jay instead. They never measured up. The way they kissed me didn't light a fire deep inside of me. My pulse didn't race. My heart didn't beat wildly in my chest.

Because they weren't Jay. They never would be.

Dating was pointless. My heart belonged to someone already and there was no way for me to take it back. I didn't want to even though I knew I should let him go. We were worlds apart, and not only separated by miles but also by the death of Sam.

I was prepared to spend the rest of my life alone. My battery-operated boyfriend got the job done. What did I need a man for anyway?

Then I answered Spencer's call, and it feels like my entire life has been turned upside down again. I came back here understanding it would be hard. Knowing today, of all days, could potentially destroy me all over again.

Yet, it hasn't.

I feel stronger. Braver.

A lot of that I have Jay to thank for. His presence has always forced me to confront my feelings and push them down deep. To smile through the pain. To find the good in a bad situation.

He doesn't know it, but every time I saw him in college I cringed internally as much as I would swoon. I would watch him when I was certain no one else was looking. Study his mannerisms, looking for flaws. Needing to find something that would change my opinion of him.

In reality, I watched him with admiration in my eyes. Not only because he's handsome but because he's kind. A good person at heart. Generous with his time. Smart.

He has a heart of gold and a soul as deep as the Grand Canyon.

Five years may have passed since I last saw him, but those things haven't changed. Neither has the way he looks at me, with lust in his eyes. They practically burn my skin as they travel the length of my body from head to toe and back again until I'm staring into his darkened hazel globes.

"We don't have time," I protest, knowing his thoughts match my own.

"Says who?" he asks, pulling me against his chest and dipping his head so he can kiss the sweet spot behind my ear.

"Says me. I need to shower or we're going to be late."

Placing my palm flat against his chest, I attempt to push out of his embrace, but he holds tight, never stopping his assault on my neck. His lips are silky smooth against my skin and I can feel the moisture pooling in my panties.

Why am I trying to deny him again?

Oh, yeah. We have a marathon to run.

Another nudge from me and Jay lifts his head, a devious grin on his face. He starts walking us backward toward the bathroom, and all I can do is smile because I know what happens next.

We get dirty before we get clean.

———

LATE SEEMS TO BE A THING WITH US. I'VE NEVER BEEN LATE A day in my life until recently. In fact, I'm the one who shows up fifteen minutes early to everything. If I'm not at least that early, I feel behind. Rushed. It's a feeling I don't like and try to avoid at all costs.

Yet, showing up late with Jay's arm wrapped around my shoulder doesn't bring about the sense of panic I expect. It could be the two mind-blowing orgasms I had in the shower. Or the third one as he bent me over the bathroom sink.

Who am I kidding?

It's all those things, but it's also the fact he held my hand the entire walk over. That when we approached, he grazed the tips of his fingers up my arm before pulling me to his side. How natural it feels to be wrapped in his embrace.

It's everything about Jay that has me feeling cool as a cucumber as we approach where Spencer is about to take the makeshift stage in the parking lot of Riley's Pub. It's nothing more than two partially broken pallets stacked on top of each other, but it gives him the advantage to look out over the still growing crowd of runners.

The beautiful spring morning is perfect for a marathon —warm enough to keep the chill off my exposed skin but the light breeze will keep me cool while running.

Taking a deep breath and letting it out slowly, I prepare myself for the words I'm about to hear. It's Spencer's turn to speak. To talk about Sam. About the impact she made on his life. I can't think of anything he could say that already hasn't been said. It's clear we all loved her. We miss her.

Her story is tragic. No one will ever dispute that fact.

I will find justice for Sam if it's the last thing I do.

"Thank you all for coming out this morning," Spencer starts. "It was an honor to have called Sam my friend and it's an honor to be here today to kick off the first annual Samantha Bridges memorial race. For five years I've walked past the park," Spence motions to the park behind the crowd of runners and all heads turn, "and it reminded me of the worst day of my life. The day I found out one of my best friends, a girl who was a ray of sunshine in everyone's life, was taken from us. Today we erase the memory of that day and remember Sam for the amazing soul she was. We're going to celebrate her. We're going to take back the parts of our heart that shattered all those years ago."

Five years.

She's been gone for five years.

It's been even longer since I've talked to my friend. Hugged her. Tried not to laugh as she pouted at me. Made fun of her for the crazy pens she would write with at work. Helped her pick out a new hair color.

The hours we used to spend together, doing nothing but talking, feel like they went by so fast, yet since she died, the days have dragged on. Life has slowed down.

Today is the hardest day of the year for me. I'm normally wrapped in a blanket on my couch with tears in my eyes. Looking at the few pictures I still have stored on my cell phone. Wondering where she would be now if she were still with us. Making up an amazing life for her.

She'd be married with kids. A boy and a girl. Her daughter would be the spitting image of her the way she resembles her mother. Her son would have her fire. She would be happy and healthy, living an adventurous life.

The chance at that life was stolen from her.

The reminder causes a chill to wash over me, my skin pebbling even though the warm morning sun is beating down on me.

"Before I officially kick off the race, I'd like to share the story of how I met Sam. As most of you know, I'm not from Great Falls even though I'm proud I now call this place home." The crowd applauds, and Spence bows, a silly grin on his face. Always the showman. Always finding a way to make people laugh. Even in times like these. Even when he's about to talk about Sam. "I was a sophomore at GFU, and I'll be honest with you, I don't remember much of my freshman year. It was a blur of parties and hangovers."

The tension in the air lifts as the crowd laughs.

"Surprisingly, I only failed one class. Freshman English, and I am horrible at English, so I needed a plan to make sure I wasn't taking it again my junior year. Picture this. I'm sitting in the back row of the classroom, contemplating my options, when in walks a girl with bright red lipstick and streaks in her hair to match. It's piled on top of her head in one of those messy ponytails all the girls wear. Class started at noon, but it looked like she had just rolled out of bed. She had a coffee in each hand and a pencil holding her hair up.

"When she plopped into the seat next to me, I knew we were going to be friends. I tried not to stare at her, but she was beautiful. Her personality was shining brightly even when her eyes were closed and I thought she fell asleep. I wanted to talk to her, but she intimidated me."

Spencer had a thing for Sam. I never would have guessed. Then again, I hadn't met them yet.

"I stalked her for two weeks after class started, waiting for the perfect moment to ask her for help. I was already behind and she seemed to sleep through class but managed to pull an A on our first exam. Then one day she turned to me and asked what my name was. I was barely able to get both syllables out before she was interrogating me about creeping on her."

This time I can't help but laugh. My body is shaking as I bend over and hold my stomach. I can hear Sam calling him out in her no-nonsense way. She didn't tolerate bullshit. She had no filter. If she was thinking it, you would hear about it. Whether you wanted to or not. No matter if she should share her thoughts or keep them to herself.

Jay runs his hand up and down my back as I straighten up. I'd almost forgotten he was next to me, Spencer's story capturing my attention. He pulls me in front of him, wrapping his arms around my waist. When I look over my shoulder, I see unshed tears glistening in his eyes. I've already wiped away two strays.

Spencer continues his story, but I can't take my eyes off of Jay's. He's holding it all in. The pain. The sorrow. The memories of a time before life was complicated. When Sam lit up our world just because she was a part of it.

"And then she fell for my roommate. The biggest mistake I ever made was introducing them. The ass was always better looking than me. Still is. I was upset with her until she brought over a friend, not wanting me to feel like the third wheel when we hung out. It was then I realized what true love was. Yes, I loved Sam, but in a different way. She was the first girl I called friend. The only girl not to fall for my bullshit pickup lines. And she cared enough to tell me when I was being a jerk. I loved that girl ... but when Mia walked in the room it was as if my heart started beating just for her. I'm just lucky she felt the same way."

I spot Mia standing next to the stage, grinning from ear to ear.

Yes, Spencer. You are very lucky. Not only that you met Sam but that she introduced you to Mia.

"Sam was a matchmaker. A coffee fiend. Pushy. Funny. Caring. Moody in the mornings but vibrant at night. She wore red lipstick proudly every single day. She had a personality that can only be described as unique. Her friendship was unconditional, and she would have done anything for anyone if they asked. Sam was a one-of-a-kind person, and she would be humbled to see how many people are here to honor her memory today. With that, I'd like to get this race started. Runners," Spence says, straightening his back and deepening his voice in a more professional manner, "please take your places."

I can't help but shake my head at my friend as Jay and I walk hand in hand toward the starting line. It's been a few years since I've run more than a mile on my treadmill, so this is going to suck. I'll be exhausted and ache in places I shouldn't but running also makes you feel alive.

Today is a good day to remember what it feels like to be alive. To live. A reminder that even though we've lost someone we love, that the pain we feel over that loss is real, we're still here.

Spencer and Mia join us at the front of the crowd. Before handing over the microphone, Spencer goes over the route with everyone.

Three laps around the central part of town basically. Follow the park north along Main street, turn east onto First and follow it down to State. Take State Street south to Second and then head west back to Main Street.

We'll be running past both Summer's house as well as the Hideaway. We'll cover three sides of the park; the one remaining side is where Sam's body was found. I haven't stepped foot in the park since she was found. I never planned to again, but today that has to change. After the race is over, we've been instructed to head to the center of the park for the fountain dedication.

The city had a small memorial fountain placed near where Sam's body was found. The weight of that reality slams into me as I hear someone blow a horn, signifying the start of the race. The crowd moves forward, spreading out once we're on the main road. Jay's long legs set the pace for the four of us but it's not long before Mia and I fall back. With an eight-inch height advantage, I was taking two strides for every one of his, both my lungs and legs burning by the time we made the turn onto State Street.

"Want to slow down?" Mia asks as we approach the parking lot of Riley's, marking the end of the first of our three laps.

"Yes, please," I say, slowing my strides until I'm briskly walking.

There are volunteers handing out cups of water to the racers and I take two, stopping to down them both before continuing on.

"How are you holding up this morning?" she asks, falling back in step with me.

"I'm doing okay. I know what today is, but for some reason it hasn't hit me as hard as it has the last few years."

"That's because you're back here with us."

"You'd think that'd make it harder. Being here. Remembering her. Celebrating her. All I've done is think about her for the last two days. I've read through that file more times than I care to count and studied pictures of her dead body. I think I'm numb to it at this point. All of it. The pain, the violence."

"I think you're finally accepting it. Think about it. The last few years were hard because you didn't want to come to terms with what happened. You tried to ignore it. That's why you thought it would be harder to be here on the anniversary but now you're surrounded by people that loved her. People who love you."

Mia makes a valid point. The last four years, when this date would begin to creep up, I've shut down emotionally. I've pushed people away, hid in my apartment, and cried over the loss of my best friend. Have I dealt with her death? Not really. I haven't had any support in healing either.

As crazy as I thought this idea was, perhaps coming

back here was a good thing. Maybe it will help me move on.

"Jay loves you," I hear Mia say as we pass Summer's house.

I avoided looking in the general direction the first lap. My lungs were burning, my chest already tight. I wasn't about to add any more stress to my body.

Wait. What?

Mia's words slam into me as I stutter, "Um, wh-what are you t-talking about?"

"Jay. Loves. You." Her words are pointed as she pulls us to a stop in the middle of the road, runners swerving to avoid crashing into us.

"Mia, it's not like that. We're just friends, that's all we've ever been." Lies. All lies. And I don't even know why I'm saying them. Even I don't believe the words coming out of my mouth.

"Friends?" she asks with a laugh. "I don't have many friends that hold me the way he holds you. Whose eyes darken with lust when I walk in the room. Whose words speak to my heart in a way that only I understand. No, the only person that feels that way about me is Spencer."

I'm at a loss for words, my mouth hanging slightly ajar, as I catch sight of Spence and Jay approaching behind us. They're deep in conversation, Spencer's hands moving animatedly while Jay shakes his head.

"I bet they're having the same conversation we are. Jay refuses to admit that he loves you. That he's always loved you. We saw it back then and we see it now."

"What do you mean back then?" I ask, turning my back to Mia and willing my legs to move. They cooperate long enough to get a few paces in front of her, but she catches up easily, my body exhausted from the distance we've already put in.

"New Year's Eve ring a bell?"

Our first kiss.

The night I betrayed my best friend and swore I would never do it again. I tried my best, separated myself, only I failed.

When I don't answer, she continues, "We all saw it. The change in you. The change in him. We knew something happened between you two. You grew distant and so did he. He locked himself in his room and took computers apart most of the time. He never wanted to hang out. Made excuses for why he couldn't spend time with anyone, including Sam.

"She saw it, you know, but not through our eyes. She was convinced she messed up. She blamed herself. Thought he wanted to break up with her because he was pushing her away. The only time we saw him after that was when you were around. His eyes would light up. He was a completely different person. Spence and I weren't surprised. We'd always known he held a candle for you but never thought he'd act on it."

"He didn't hold a candle for me. That's such a stupid saying," I retort as we pass the volunteers with water, marking the start of our final lap. Jay and Spencer are standing only a few feet away, talking with Summer, already finished with their final lap.

"He told Spencer about you before he knew who you were."

fifteen

SUDDENLY I'M PROPELLING TOWARD THE GROUND. THE moment I first met Jay flashing before my eyes. The feel of his arm wrapped around me as he stopped me from falling on the sidewalk. The heat in my cheeks when I realized my underwear were scattered on the grass.

His smile.

The damn dimple.

The blue specks shining against the backdrop of his hazel eyes.

A warmth wraps around my body as I'm pulled upright and against a hard body. A body I know intimately. A chest I traced with my tongue earlier this morning before I properly thanked him for bringing me coffee.

Coffee I never drank because I was too busy thanking him.

"Gotta watch out for those pebbles," Jay whispers in my ear, kissing the nape of my neck before releasing me and sauntering away, back to where Spencer is waiting with a smirk on his face.

"Still want to deny it?" Mia asks, nudging me in the side as we watch the guys walk into the park, Jay's arm wrapped around Summer's shoulder.

"Does it really matter what may or may not have happened five years ago? It's history."

Even I don't believe the lies I'm trying to sell her. It may be in the past, but I still don't think I can bring myself to confess my sins out loud.

"He scares you that much, huh?"

"I'm not scared of Jay," I start, picking up the pace so we can finish the race sooner rather than later. "He's a great guy, but he was Sam's boyfriend—"

"Was."

"And she died. They would still be together if she was alive."

"Do you really believe that?"

No. I can't admit that to her, though. I can't tell her he told me he was planning on breaking up with her.

"The fact you won't even answer tells me all I need to know," Mia says, letting silence descend upon us.

I'm waiting for her to say something else. However, as we approach the finish line, she still hasn't. Not a single word. For Mia, that's a record of silence. Especially when her opinion is weighing heavy on her.

"Just say it. I know you're thinking something," I urge as I pull her over to a bench just outside of the park.

"I believe you two love each other. I think you always have, and that you repressed those feelings because you also loved Sam. When she died, you ran. Away from here. Away from us. You also ran away from Jay, the one person who you should have been running toward. You didn't because you think Sam would be pissed. You feel like you betrayed her by falling in love with Jay, but what you don't realize is that she wouldn't have been angry with you. If she had known how you both felt, she would have stepped aside.

"Did she love him? Yes, but it wasn't the kind of love I feel for Spence. It wasn't the 'I want to marry you and have ten kids and grow old with you' kind of love. It was fun and exciting, and he made her feel special."

Would she have understood?

Maybe in the beginning, if we'd been honest with her. That first night when she introduced us. If I'd come clean and confessed I'd met Jay before. That I found him attractive. That there was an undeniable chemistry between us. But not after two years, though. Not after all the pretending we did. All the lies of omission.

I let Mia's words sink in as I think back over the last few weeks I spent with Sam before she was killed, searching my mind for any clues that she knew what was going on. That she saw more than I thought she did.

She talked a lot about Jay those few weeks. Asking my opinion on the situation. She always came to me for relationship advice, though. That wasn't abnormal.

Did I give myself away with my answers?

———

"He's acting strange again. I asked him if he wanted to go to the late showing at the theater last night and he never texted me back. I ended up going by myself, sitting in the back row, and crying through what was supposed to be a thriller."

My gut is to laugh at the vivid image my mind has concocted of Sam bawling while someone on the screen is being chased with a chainsaw, but I hold it in. Tuck it down deep. Just like the rest of my feelings. Because right now she needs her best friend. She needs a shoulder to cry on.

"Why'd you go alone?" I ask, already knowing the answer. If Sam wants to do something, she doesn't need anyone to do it with her. She'll go alone, no matter how pathetic she might think it looks.

"You were working. Plus, I wasn't really alone. I mean, there were other people there, I just wasn't sitting with them. Well, Ben did come over to check on me when he saw I was crying. He didn't say anything, just handed me a box of tissues and offered to refill my popcorn for me."

"The owner?" I know exactly who she's talking about.

"Yeah. I dated his younger brother in high school for a little while. I was a freshman, and Brandon was a senior. He was the smart one, and Ben was the screw up back then. Ben was good at sports but not much else. I was surprised when he took over the business for his parents when his dad got sick a few years ago. If Brandon and Ruth hadn't bought the Hideaway, I bet Brandon would have taken over the theater."

"That was nice of him to check on you, but next time, don't go to the movies alone. Just come see me at work or something if you want to hang out. You know Mindi will break all the rules and let you sit at the bar and drink as long as Riley's not there."

Riley's never there anymore. Not past five in the afternoon anyway. If Mindi is in the building, she runs the show. Hell, she runs the show even if Riley is around. Everyone knows it.

"You never hang out anymore," Sam complains, tossing the magazine she's been browsing through on my coffee table before running her fingers through her hair. The tips are teal right now. She said my new chair inspired the change. The chair she's sitting in even though it's the most uncomfortable piece of shit I've ever owned. "It's like I'm cursed. You're busy with school and Jay's busy tearing apart every computer he can get his hands on. What happens when both of you graduate in a few months? I'm going to be left here with no friends."

"Mia and Spence are going to be here." I'm not sure why I feel the need to point this out.

"Is that your way of telling me you won't be here?"

I haven't confirmed I'm leaving but I've never tried to hide *the fact either. My plan was never to stay in Great Falls. I came here for school, and with a degree in psychology, it'll be easy to find a job back home. Here? Not so much.*

"*You know I've always planned to go back to LA for work. It'll be easier to get a job there than here.*"

"*Jay's already said he's planning on going back to Virginia.*" *My back stiffens at the mention of him leaving and I avert my eyes back toward my laptop.*

Did she catch the slight shift? Was she looking in my direction? I really hope not. I used to be good at hiding my reactions from her but after three months of spending time apart, I'm starting to slip.

"*This town doesn't have much to offer beyond an education. Don't take it personal, Sam. You can always come visit; you know that. It'll give you an excuse to travel. You love going on epic adventures.*"

I use her own words against her and I don't even feel bad about it. She showed up at my apartment in the middle of me studying for a test on my night off. A test she knows is a big chunk of my final grade. It can make or break this class for me. As much as I've been using school as an excuse, I was actually busy tonight.

"*Right. Epic adventures.*" *Her voice lacks emotion, but I don't bother to look up, avoiding eye contact with her so she doesn't see through my lies. What I'm really worried about is her seeing the guilt in my eyes.*

"*How much longer do you have? Want to take a break and walk over to Jay's apartment with me? Maybe if we show up together we can get him to take a break from whatever he has his hands on and spend time with us.*"

His hands have been on me, *I think to myself.*

I want to say the words aloud. To confess my sins to her. Instead, I shake my head and keep my eyes trained on the screen

in front of me. The words are blurring together the harder I stare,
my thoughts drifting to the fact Jay is leaving after graduation.
Not just leaving Great Falls. Leaving Sam.

———

My gut tells me that if she didn't know, she suspected something. She had to. Sam wasn't stupid, and we were both acting distant.

Taking my hand, Mia gives it a little squeeze. "She loved you, Andi. You were her best friend. She would want you to be happy. She wouldn't resent you for falling in love with Jay. And, most of all, she would want you to be with someone who loves you as much as you love them. Someone who can help you heal from your loss. Who understands you and accepts you for the person you are."

Mia's given me a lot to think about at a time where I already have enough running through my mind. Yes, I can hear everything she's saying. I believe her. She may be the only other person who knew and understood Sam as well as I did. That doesn't make the guilt any less palpable.

Or my heart any less broken.

It's beat for Jay for years, and as much as I'd like to hold onto the way I feel when I'm in his arms, I don't know if I'm strong enough. No matter how you spin it, it still feels like betrayal.

All I can do is nod my head, over and over again, as Mia stares at me, waiting for me to reply. The words won't come. I can't even muster the strength to agree or disagree with her.

Instead, I stand and turn toward the entrance to the park. Taking a deep breath and letting it out slowly, I put on a brave face and put one foot in front of the other.

Maybe in another life we could have been together.

Perhaps if I'd met him first.

If he'd chosen me over Sam the night she introduced us.

People like to use the phrase 'what a difference a day makes'.

Sometimes it's not even a day. One single defining moment can change everything.

It doesn't do me any good to dwell on the past, on the what-ifs. Nothing will change what happened back then and the past has brought us to this point right now. Standing inside of the park where my best friend was murdered. Where I'll stand next to the man that was her boyfriend when she died, hold his hand, and listen as her mother shares stories of her only daughter.

As I slide up next to Jay, he wraps his arm around me, kissing the top of my head. He's still sweaty from the race, the light gray shirt he wore this morning now splattered with dark splotches, clinging to his chest.

He needs another shower, and I will gladly volunteer to wash his back. And every other part of him.

Because in twenty-four hours, I'm going to lose him all over again. He'll head back to wherever he lives now, and I'll be on a plane to LA. It's our last official night together and I plan to make the most out of it. I'm going to ignore the guilt that feels like it's crushing my soul.

"Anyone want coffee?" Spence asks, appearing in front of us freshly showered.

"Yes, please," I say, jumping away from Jay as if we were caught sucking face instead of cuddling.

Spence raises an eyebrow at me but doesn't call me out, instead motioning for me to follow him when both Mia and Jay decline his offer. Not before he shares a knowing look with Mia though. Not before I catch her hint of a smile.

As the crowd thins around us, I notice a few vendors set up near the playground. Large banners cover the front of the tables, extension cords winding through the grass behind them. We're headed straight for the Java Bean's table.

"Two mochas, please," Spence say when it's our turn to order, handing over cash to one girl as the other starts making our drinks.

The cashier winks at Spencer when she hands him back his change, but he doesn't appear to notice. He drops a few singles in the tip jar and takes my elbow, leading us to a bench to wait for our order.

"Did Mia talk to you?" he asks once we're seated.

"You know damn well she did. I think you guys are tag teaming us."

"We may have a plan."

"What's the bet this time?"

"No bet, Beauty Queen. This isn't about being right or wrong. We're both on the same side. We want you two to be happy."

There are many sides to Spencer, but he generally only shows one. He's the funny guy. The prankster. The one who would bet on anything against anyone, even if the odds were stacked against him. He makes light of all situations and tries not to take life too seriously.

Right now, he's using an authoritative voice with me. One that makes me feel small beneath his stare. If this is how he is with suspects when interrogating them, I wouldn't be surprised if he has an impeccable record for confessions.

"I appreciate what you two are trying to do," I state,

standing when they call our order, "but save yourself the trouble. Let's just enjoy the last day we have together. I'm almost finished with the profile and I'm meeting with the chief tomorrow at noon on my way out of town. You should be there. I want you to hear it. Then, I'm headed back to Cali. Back to the life I've built there. I'll miss you guys. This town will always hold a special place in my heart, but I won't be coming back.

"It's too much to take. Too many memories around every corner, and though ninety-nine percent of them are good memories, the end result is still the same. My heart breaks all over again. The day I found out she was killed slaps me across the face and I'm right back to where I started. Mourning the loss of my best friend."

"But—"

"Spence, I love you. You're a great friend, and I promise to call more often. You and Mia can come visit me in LA but as far as everything else goes, I'm leaving it all here. I'm moving on. Letting go as best I can. It might not be what I want but it's what I need."

Spence only nods as he hands me my mocha, wraps his arm around my shoulder, and guides us back into the crowd in search of the rest of our group. My tribe. The people I'll always be able to turn to because they're the only other people who understand what I've been through.

sixteen

"As an only child, Sam knew how to get what she wanted from me. We didn't have a lot of money and I was always working, but it was almost as if she knew when to ask. I'd come home from work after a twelve-hour shift, be ready to close my eyes from exhaustion, and this ray of sunshine would walk in the room with a huge smile on her face and strike." Summer chuckles at the memory as tears begin to form in my eyes.

I'd seen Sam work her magic on Summer on more than one occasion.

"I couldn't tell her no, even when I should have. The way her smile grew, lighting up the room, was what I lived for. Every day of my life I lived for that child. To make her happy. To hear her laugh. To watch her grow into the vibrant, young woman she was. The last conversation I had with Sam was about her hair. If you knew her well, you knew how much she loved to experiment. She was ready for her friends to get back from spring break so she could change her hair. Again.

"She was debating between hot pink and dark blue. We were fighting over which color she should go with and, per usual, Sam decided she could make the decision for us by flipping a coin. Heads she would go blue, tails pink. When it landed on heads she frowned and said she had to do best of three or it didn't count. She wanted to get her way, but she wanted luck to be on her side as well.

"You see, she believed in things like that. Luck. Fate. She believed that things happened for a reason. And at that moment, that if her hair was meant to be pink, the coin would land on tails twice. Of course, it did. She kissed me on the cheek and bounced out of the house minutes later, heading in for her shift at Riley's."

Summer pauses, and I let out the breath I didn't even realize I was holding. I wasn't there for their conversation, but I could picture it in my mind. The frown on Sam's face when the coin landed on heads. The joy when pink was the ultimate winner. The pep in her step as she walked to work.

The little victories brought her the most joy.

"If I had known that would have been the last time I would see my daughter, I would have hugged her a little tighter. Held her longer. Kissed her one last time. I would have poured my entire heart into that good-bye. But, like Sam, I also believe everything happens for a reason. That even though it hurts, her death was not in vain. It was meant to happen and there was nothing we could do to stop it.

"It's hard to hold onto that feeling after all this time. Without knowing who or why. Without closure. But for Sam, I'm holding on. I'm trying my best to wake up every day and live the life I've been given. To believe that fate is still at work. That even though I don't understand it, her death has a significance we've yet to figure out."

Summer closes her eyes for a moment, her hand visibly shaking as she holds the microphone to her mouth. Before I realize what I'm doing, I'm standing next to Summer on the stage, taking her other hand in mine and giving it a squeeze.

"Sam would have been so proud of you," she says into the microphone, but her words are directed at me. "She's smiling down on all of us, guiding us each and every day. Toward our futures. Toward our destiny. But you, Andrea, she's walking by your side. I know it. You were the sister she always wanted. Her other half. When you two were together, you couldn't tell where one of you ended and the other began. It was as if you were one person. Fate brought you together. She told me that once. She was feeling lost, and you walked in the door and everything felt right again.

"I may have lost my biological daughter five years ago today, but I'm grateful I still have you. I'm grateful for all of Sam's friends. Without Spencer and Mia, I wouldn't be as strong as I am. There are days I wasn't able to pull myself out of bed, and there they were, forcing me to go on. A mother's grief is indescribable. I don't wish it on my worst enemy. No one should ever have to bury their child, but if the unfortunate happens, I pray they have a family of people who love them to pull them through."

Tears are freely streaming down my face when Summer faces the crowd again. They're all staring at me but the only person I see is Jay, standing in the back, smiling at me with tears glistening in his eyes.

"Before we reveal the fountain," Summer continues, gesturing to the large object covered in a black sheet next to me, "I'd like to thank the community of Great Falls for rallying around me. For caring about my daughter as if she was their own. For helping in every way in an attempt to find out who did this to her. To bring justice for Sam. We will find out one day, and it will be because the love we all have for her kept us going. Pushing forward."

Summer turns off the mic, dropping her arm at her side, as she nods to Spencer who's moved to stand next to the statue. He gives the covering a tug, and the black sheet falls away, revealing a large sculpture. Four thin, stainless-steel beams bending and twisting around each other, reaching toward the sky. It stands in the middle of a large, square basin that's filled with water.

Moments later, the water begins to move, shooting straight up through the four beams. The water rides back down on the steel, causing it to shimmer in the early afternoon light.

It's gorgeous. A great representation of Sam and the way she touched everyone around her with her light.

"Thank you all so much for coming out today to celebrate Sam's life. She would have been touched to know you all care. Please feel free to throw a coin in the fountain and make a wish. I'd like to believe Sam will make an effort to grant it for you."

The crowd applauds Summer as she waves at them when they begin dispersing—some toward the vendors, others to get a better look at the fountain. I'm frozen in place, watching as everyone goes on with their lives. Knowing a life was taken in this very spot five years ago, the weight of why I'm here pressing against my chest.

The urge to run is overwhelming. To get in my rental car and never look back. Change my phone number and disappear. To curl up under the covers of my bed and cry the way I have for the last few years.

But you can't outrun your past. It's bound to catch up to you. The memories can't be erased. They travel with you wherever you go. They're a part of you, ingrained in you. They've made me who I am today.

The good and the bad.

Even the unforgivable memories have impacted me.

"Thank you again, Andi," I hear Summer say, her words louder than I expect them to be. "Knowing you're helping the police gives me a renewed sense of hope."

The microphone. She didn't turn it off.

"If there's any chance of finding out who did this after all this time, I think this might be it."

When I glance over my shoulder, I find everyone's attention is focused on us again. They've stopped their retreat and are making their way back toward the stage. I'm frozen in place, sharing a petrified look with Jay as he pushes his way through the crowd, but that doesn't stop Summer from talking.

"I appreciate everything you're doing. You and Jay. Spencer's been working so hard to—"

Summer's words are cut off from the crowd as Spencer pulls the microphone from Summer's hand and flips the switch. Her head jerks around in surprise to find Jay and Spencer staring down at her with a look of fear on their faces.

"We need to talk. In private. My house. Twenty minutes." Spencer's words are clipped, his tone even more serious than the one he took with me earlier. Anger is vibrating off his body in waves as Mia slides up next to him, taking his hand and pulling him away.

Summer's still staring after him in shock when Jay places his hand on her shoulder. "It's going to be okay. I promise."

"What did I just do?" she asks, tears welling in her eyes.

"You gave away the element of surprise, but that doesn't mean we won't still be able to catch him." Jay's voice softens as he pulls Summer to his chest, holding her close as she sobs.

We stand like that far longer than I'm comfortable. Jay's eyes are focused on me as he holds Summer. I'm staring back at him, sending up a silent prayer that things aren't about to fall apart. That I didn't just spend the last two days working my ass off for things to blow up in my face tomorrow.

There are still people lingering around, watching us with interest, when Jay finally releases Summer, stepping up next to me and whispering in my ear, "If he was here, he knows we're looking for him. Did you recognize anyone?"

Everyone. I recognized almost everyone. Most of the crowd were local business owners, members of the community. People I had interacted with while I lived her. Served drinks to at Riley's.

"We need to get to Spencer's and work damage control," is all I say before I walk off the stage and head across the park to where I know a very angry Spencer will be pacing his apartment, waiting on us to arrive.

As if predicting the future, I find Mia in her kitchen, pouring shots, while Spencer walks the length of their living room, hands fisted at his side, cursing under his breath. His anger is palpable, his footsteps causing the floor to vibrate.

"It could be worse," I state, flopping down on their couch, but he doesn't stop his travels.

"How?"

"Well, for starters, she could have said we were looking for someone local. Though, I did hint at that the other night, so if he was at the lantern release, he might already know that. Or that I was creating a profile. No one knows what I do for a living. Hell, they may think we're just nosing around because we loved Sam."

"I'm a police officer, Andrea." The use of my full name

catches my attention, and when I look over the back of the couch, I find Spencer standing, arms crossed over his chest, shooting daggers in my direction. "She mentioned my name. Whoever he is, he's been silent the last five years. I've run every angle. I never talk about it though. No one does. If he was there and he heard what Summer said—"

"Don't blame Summer," Jay interrupts. "She didn't know the microphone was on. She wasn't trying to give him an unfair advantage."

"I'm sorry." Summer's voice is small as she bows her head from her place next to Mia at the island.

"I'm not mad at you," Spencer starts, taking a step in her direction, but stops when Mia shakes her head once in warning. "I'm pissed because this asshole knows we're looking for him again and we're close to figuring out who he is. The last thing I want is for him to get away with it."

"He won't," I assure Spence, pushing off the couch and moving to stand in front of him. "I'm finishing the profile tonight and delivering it tomorrow. Someone is bound to recognize who it is. Someone will know, and then we'll have him. He can try and run but he won't. He's too conceited. He thinks because he's gotten away with it this long, he'll never get caught. Besides, running will only make him look guilty."

"Are you sure?" he questions, his eyes penetrating mine with such an intense stare I step back.

"Trust me. I know what I'm doing. I'm damn good at my job and I don't plan to give up until he's caught. If that means I'm staying here until that happens, so be it." Mimicking his stance, I cross my arms over my chest and glare at Spencer.

"Is that supposed to be a threat?" Mia asks. Glancing over my shoulder to where she now has one arm wrapped around Summer and the other is holding an empty shot glass, she smirks at me.

"Not a threat, a promise. I don't plan on leaving until we have answers. I can't run away again."

Her eyes flick to Spencer's briefly before returning to mine, her smile growing.

"You don't have to sacrifice your life, Andi," Summer whispers, but I don't take my eyes off Mia.

"It's not a sacrifice. I want to help. I need to help. None of us will truly have closure until the person responsible is caught. There are people in this town who can't even look out their windows without being reminded of what happened. People who can't sleep at night knowing he's still out there." I pause and suck in a deep breath to ensure I don't lose my composure. "I'm sick of dreaming about that night. Of feeling guilty for missing my flight. Of blaming myself because there's no one else to blame. This wasn't my fault. Or anyone else's. There's one person responsible for what happened that night and they need to be held accountable so the rest of us can feel like we're able to breathe again."

The room falls silent at my admission.

I've been suffering in silence. Alone, for five long years, and I'm done pretending nothing happened. That I don't feel partially to blame even though I'm not the one who took her life.

"If you're to blame, so am I," Spencer says, pulling my attention away from Mia as she pours herself another shot.

"How so?"

"I could have drove her home that night. We were back in town but didn't tell anyone. We wanted one last night for just the two of us," he explains, averting his eyes to the wood floor beneath his feet. "I was selfish. I knew she'd have to walk, and even though it was nice that night, didn't offer to pick her up. A good friend would have at least offered."

"A good boyfriend would have been there, so you didn't have to," Jay chimes in as he approaches Spence, placing his hand on his shoulder.

"None of you are to blame," Summer's voice booms. I've never heard her yell before, so the deep timber of her voice catches me off guard. All eyes fall to her as she steps around the island and points at the three of us before continuing, "If you're guilty of anything it's loving my daughter. Of caring for her. Sam believed everything happens for a reason, and right now, I need you to believe as well. It's the only thing that's gotten me through this. Her death was tragic, it almost killed me, but it happened, and we may never know what the reason was. However, we can start by finding the asshole responsible."

Summer's hand flies to her lips.

I've never seen her so angry. Never heard her swear. She's never needed to. If she has a point to make, she can do it without getting worked up or shouting profanities.

We all know this, which is why the four of us can't help but laugh. Mia's the first to break, her laughter echoing off the walls of the loft. I follow suit, and the guys aren't far behind me. Summer's face is bright red, but she soon joins us.

As our laughter begins to fade, the mood in the room shifts again. It's heavy. Realization settling in.

"I'd feel better if we caught a break. I don't care how small; anything is better than nothing. Hell, if we could find her apron, I'd fucking run naked through town with a smile on my face." Spencer's voice cuts through the tension like a knife.

"Her apron?" I ask as his words sink in, my mind running a mile a minute, attempting to remember if it was mentioned in the files anywhere.

"It wasn't with her. They think he took it with him," Spencer explains.

"A trophy," I whisper to myself. The words are barely out when I realize what we're missing, my head whipping in Jay's direction. When our eyes meet, he nods and we're out the door without looking back.

seventeen

"HOW DID I MISS THIS?" I ASK, SCANNING THROUGH THE pages of Sam's file for anything else I may have overlooked. I'm pissed at myself. I've always prided myself on the little details. I'm usually able to see things no one else can.

This case, because it's Sam, has me feeling less and less like the strong, smart, intuitive woman I normally am.

"It wasn't noted in the file. You can look all you want. You didn't miss anything, Drea. They left that detail out. I don't even know how Spencer figured it out. I would have asked but I saw the look in your eye. I wasn't about to let you walk anywhere alone after Summer's confession. She put a target on your back. On all our backs."

"He wouldn't strike in broad daylight," I retort, brushing off Jay's concerns, but there's a nagging feeling crawling on my skin that my assumption is wrong.

If he feels we're getting close, he might do something out of character. It could be anything from starting a fight to getting wasted and driving. Or something bigger, more aggressive, like kill again. Not necessarily me but whoever is his current object of obsession.

Should we warn the chief?

The thought crosses my mind, but I cancel it out. The town is going to be crawling with people tonight.

"We have no idea who this guy is. The last thing I want to do is risk losing you."

Flipping the page, I find the information I was searching for, holding the page above my head and smiling up at Jay who's looking at me like I've lost my mind.

"Care to share?"

"This is the list of people they initially eliminated."

He looks at me as if to say "And?"

"Think about this. He kills Sam, takes her apron, and has to hide it. He can't take it home because if he's questioned, they might search his place. He's not going to throw it away, he needs to be able to see it, to touch it. It's a trophy of his accomplishment. Like I said before, if he couldn't have Sam, no one could. Her apron proves that. He made it happen."

"So, if it's not at his place but he held onto it, where would he put it?"

"That's the kicker. No one would suspect him so he could have put it anywhere." My excitement is growing as the smile fades from Jay's lips, his dimple disappearing.

"Which makes us no closer to finding it than we were before we knew it was missing."

"Actually, that's not true. Okay, think about this. I'm going to use you as an example because you were cleared of any involvement." He raises his eyebrow but nods for me to continue. "If you had killed her and taken the apron, you wouldn't have brought it back to your place. You would have taken it somewhere and hid it. Somewhere you went often and could revisit it without bringing suspicion. Where would you have taken it?"

"Probably Spencer's."

"Exactly. This person has somewhere they go regularly in town. A close friend's. A family home."

"Their business?"

"No. If they were suspected of being involved, their business would be searched as well. It would have to be a place where they could hide the apron out of sight. They'd know it well; like the place they grew up."

"I get what you're saying. I grew up in a historic home, a lot like this one, and there were little nooks everywhere. There was this panel in the closet under the stairs that you could pop off and I'd hide in there when I played hide and go seek with my cousins. They never found me."

"Something like that."

"You're basically reinforcing the idea that he's from town. How do we narrow it down? If it were me, I'd be searching their computers and browser history. Even now you can find a trail that could lead us to suspicious behavior. I can't do that without a short list of suspects. We need to narrow it down to only a few people."

"I thought you worked for the government?" I asked, confused by his sudden interest in what used to be his hobby.

"I do. That doesn't mean I don't still tinker with computers. And my hacking abilities are a lot better than they used to be."

Raising an eyebrow at his confession, I wait for Jay to expand on his statement, but he doesn't. Instead, he takes the list from my hand, sets it next to the preliminary profile I wrote out in my notebook, and begins eliminating potential suspects.

Too old.

Too stupid.

Too quiet and reserved.

"That leaves us with ten people still."

"Ten is better than twenty-two," I say, reading over our

list, wondering if I'm staring at the name of the man who took my friend's life.

I know all of them.

They are all regulars at Riley's. I've seen and talked to most of them since returning to town. A few were at the lantern release, some at the brunch, but all ten were at the fountain dedication. All ten were staring at me on stage while Summer thanked me for helping. I remember the expressions on each of their faces. None of them stood out. They were all smiling up at me with hope in their eyes. Or at least that's what I thought I saw.

The big test will be if any of them show up for drinks at Riley's tonight. Everyone's invited. It's the last event for Sam's memorial celebration. The anniversary of her death.

A day that would hold special meaning to him. One he would celebrate every year. He would have a tradition. He'd visit the place he killed her. At the time he killed her. He wouldn't be able to help it. He'd be compelled to go back to the scene even though she's not there. The blood is long gone and there's no trace of what happened.

"He'll be there tonight," I say to Jay as I pull my T-shirt over my head. I'm sticky from sweating all day and need to shower before we head to Riley's. "Then he won't. He'll go back to where it all started, and I plan to be there for it."

Jay's eyes watch me intently as I pull my yoga pants off, tossing them in the corner. Slowly backing away from where he's seated on the bed, you'd think I had him tied to a string. He stands, stripping his own clothes off as he follows me into the bathroom.

"I'm going to the park tonight. I'm going to see for myself who killed Sam."

"The hell you are!" Jay roars, quickly making his way to

me and pulling me into his arms. My underwear is the only thing separating out bodies until Jay reaches down and rips them away with one tug. "You aren't going anywhere. Especially not alone. He'll give himself away, and when he does, we'll make sure he's caught. But first …" His voice trails off as his hands glide lower until they're under my ass and he's lifting me in the air.

I automatically wrap my legs around his waist, crossing my ankles, and holding on as he steps into the shower, effortlessly carrying me with him. The cold spray does nothing to cool my skin as it beats down against me.

"You were saying?" I ask, wiggling against his growing erection.

Letting out a growl, Jay lifts me with one arm, positions himself at my entrance, and enters me in one thrust, my back hitting the shower wall at the same moment his balls slap against my ass.

Our groans mix as Jay captures my lips, sliding in and out of me slowly but with such force I'm clawing at his back, wanting him closer. Needing more.

His hands come up to caress my cheeks, holding my face captive as he slows our kiss before finally pulling away, driving into me and stilling.

"I can't lose you again, Drea. I won't survive it. You can't run from me this time. Promise me you won't."

I can't promise him anything. I won't leave until I know Sam's memory can rest in peace, but as far as everything else … I just can't promise to not run away from him. Right now we need each other, but that might change once this ends.

My body is trapped against his. He's deep inside of me, waiting for me to answer him. I wrap my legs tighter around his waist, silently begging him with my eyes to move, but he doesn't budge. He wants an answer and he's not negotiating.

"I need you, Jay."

"What do you need from me?" he asks, pressing deeper though I didn't think it was possible.

"Just you. You're all I've ever needed. All I've ever wanted," I confess, the lies I was planning on telling him a forgotten thought.

I need Jay. I've always needed him. Wanted him. Craved him.

"You won't run?"

"Only if you catch me."

"I'll always catch you, Drea." Pulling back, Jay thrusts into me with punishing force. "I was meant to catch you." Another torturous thrust and I can feel the pressure building in my core. "From the moment I laid eyes on you I knew you were it for me."

Two thrusts this time and I feel him grow inside of me, my walls clenching against him as he drags across sensitive skin.

"Mine."

"Yours," I echo.

"You. Were. Made. For. Me." Each word is punctuated with a thrust until he finally stills inside of me, buried deep. The growl that escapes his lips sends me over the edge, my orgasm spiraling as I dig my nails into Jay's back.

"You own me, Drea. Heart and soul. You always have." Placing my hand against his chest, I can feel the rapid beating of Jay's heart against my palm as he rests his forehead against mine.

We stay like that for a few minutes, our bodies intertwined as we both come down from our orgasms.

"Now," he begins as he pulls his clothes back on after we've both showered off the sweat and scent of sex from our bodies, "there will be no more talk of going into the park tonight. I have a better plan."

"Of course you do."

"I need to put on clean clothes first and get ready. You should stay naked and wait in bed for me to return."

Tempting. So very tempting.

"I'm already cold," I retort, reaching into my suitcase for a sweater, the damp towel around my body sending a shiver up my spine when air kicks out of the vent at my feet.

"I promise to warm you up," he replies, wiggling his eyebrows at me as he slowly backs out of my room, barely opening the door enough to slip his large body through the opening before disappearing.

I've managed to slip into a bra and clean underwear, tossing my shredded ones in the garbage, when I hear the door to my room open. I'm standing in the bathroom, looking at myself in the mirror, contemplating my recent decisions. It's only been a few minutes since Jay left me, so when the hairs on the back of my neck stand on end, I cower behind the partially closed door and peek into the room.

He's sitting on my bed. Phone in hand. Tapping the screen without a care in the world.

"How the hell did you get back here so fast?" I ask.

We haven't talked much about where he's been staying. I know it's close, because he's never gone that long, but he's been sleeping here so I never really gave it much thought.

"It's a short walk next door," he says without looking at me. "Aren't you supposed to be naked?"

"I am," I reply flippantly as I pull my sweater over my

head with a grunt. "You're staying next door? I thought this was the only B&B on the street."

"It is."

"Who lives next door?"

"Hell if I know."

"Jay," I say, a tone of warning in my voice as I draw his name out.

"What?" he asks, finally looking up at me. When he bats his eyes at me, pleading innocence, I rest my hands on my hips and shake my head at him. "Fine. I'm staying in the room next door."

It all starts to click. It was him outside of my door that first night. He knew when I was awake because he could probably hear my alarm clock. He's never gone more than a few minutes to change. And he brought me coffee in Hideaway mugs this morning. I guarantee Brandon Royal would have had a fit if he saw someone off the street helping themselves to his coffee station that early in the morning.

"All this time you've been right next door?"

"No. I've been right here. With you. I'm just renting the room next door. If I'd known you planned to take me captive, I wouldn't have bothered to let Spencer make a reservation for me."

"Spencer?"

That little shit. He's been pulling the strings this entire time. Playing puppet master.

"Speaking of Spencer," I continue, stepping into a pair of black, skinny jeans and almost toppling over in the process. If the desk hadn't been within reach, I would have landed in a heap on the floor. "Why are he and Mia both under the impression that we're in love with each other?"

"Aren't we? Haven't we loved each other silently for years, denying our feelings to avoid hurting other people's feelings?"

I open my mouth to deny his words. To rip them apart and throw them in the garbage with the underwear he tore from my body. However, no words come out as I stare at Jay. His eyes are watching me, waiting for me to confess my deepest, darkest sins and set myself free.

Something I swore I would never do.

"I love you, Andrea. I have since the moment you fell into my arms. Before I knew anything about you, I was drawn to you. Your classic beauty, blonde hair, and deep sapphire eyes. It was your soul that spoke to me that day, though. It wrapped itself around my heart. I knew instantly that I loved you. There wasn't a doubt in my mind, and you know who was waiting for me when I walked in my apartment that afternoon? Spencer.

"He took one look at me and asked who you were. He hadn't seen us. Didn't know we'd met. He saw I was a changed man. I didn't even know your name and I was ready to drop to one knee. He saw love in its rarest form. He also saw the devastation on my face when I brought Sam home that night. And when I told him about you, about who you were, he encouraged me to be honest with Sam. To be honest with you. To break it off with her and follow my heart."

"But you were a good guy and you didn't want to hurt her."

"I didn't want to hurt either of you, and I knew if I took Spencer's advice, no one would win. So, yes, Drea, I love you. I have for years. I always will. I can't explain it any better than that. I never believed in love at first sight before I met you, but I know what I felt in that moment, what I still feel every time I look at you."

"And what's that?" I ask, finally forcing my leg into my forgotten jeans and righting myself.

"Home. I feel like I'm home. Like my soul is at peace because it's found it's match."

eighteen

Jay's words are a lot to process. The fact that he feels the same way I do has my heart wanting to do a little dance and hide at the same time. It's scary, knowing the one person in the world you want to be with, the one person you've always wanted to be with, wants to be with you, too.

It's like winning the lottery.

Overwhelming. Exciting.

There's a giant check with a bunch of zeros. A million things run through your mind. What you'll do with the money. How different your life will be now.

Then realization smacks you in the face.

You can't cash that check, it's just for show.

The money … it's real but it's dangerous.

That new life you're envisioning, do you really deserve it?

Doubt has worked its way into my mind, and in true Andrea fashion, I do what I do best.

I change the subject.

"I think we have it," I state, buttoning my pants, turning away, and beginning to refold and pack my suitcase. "The profile is as strong as it can get. We know who he is, and hopefully after I deliver it tomorrow, we'll know his name as well."

The bed creaks and a shiver runs up my spine as he approaches. My body tenses when he wraps his arms around my waist and pulls me back against his firm chest.

"Do you remember the time it snowed?"

I nod my head but remain silent.

"I was walking across campus and flakes started falling from the sky. I remember thinking how amazing it was. It was the first and only time it snowed in the four years I'd been here. It wasn't even that cold out. The snow hit the ground and melted on contact."

I remember that day. School had only been back in session for a week and I was already stressed about graduation. It wasn't the first time I'd seen snow in my life, but you would think it was by how I reacted. I was in awe as Sam and I exited the student center. She threw her bag to the ground and started spinning around in a circle, tongue hanging out, attempting to catch the tiny flakes. While it excited her, it calmed me.

"As beautiful as the snow was, do you know what was even more striking? You," he says, not bothering to wait for me to answer. "Sam was spinning around, laughing, but you were just standing there. Arms stretched out wide, face to the sky. You looked like an angel in your puffy white coat, the sun spotlighting you. There was a look of pure content on your face. Peace. I fell in love with you a little more that day."

Shaking away the memory, I attempt to pull out of his embrace, but he only tightens his hold.

"Are you coming with me tomorrow when I give the profile?" I ask.

"Then there was the time Sam and Mia dragged you on stage for karaoke. I could tell you were nervous. You were biting your bottom lip, sucking it between your teeth and fidgeting with your hair. When the song started it was like your confidence exploded on the stage. The three of you started shaking it to Taylor Swift and all your worries seemed to fade away. It was a side of you I'd rarely seen, and I fell a little more that night."

That night feels like it was a lifetime ago. It was the end of summer. I was about to start my final year of college, and Sam was hellbent on getting me up on stage. I tried to reason with her, considering my singing voice was atrocious, but she wasn't taking no for an answer. She never did.

I had no idea Jay was there that night.

Not that it would have mattered at the time. It was either get on stage or listen to Sam bitch for two weeks. Shaking my ass won out, and I pulled Mia up there to take some of the attention away from me.

When I don't comment, Jay continues down memory lane, "The night you and Sam broke the ping pong table the first time I almost lost it. I was angry with her for getting so drunk, but I was also concerned she was taking you down with her. And I blamed myself. When you two almost fell, I freaked out. Had Spencer not pulled me aside and calmed me down, I would have lost my shit in front of everyone. There would have been no denying how I felt after that.

"But it was New Year's Eve when I finally decided to stop hiding from the way I felt about you. You walked in my apartment in that little black dress. It sparkled in the light, hugged your body in all the right places. The dip in the back had my hands itching to touch you. You looked so sexy I had a wicked hard-on all night. I kept adjusting the front of my pants, thinking someone would notice. But you seemed oblivious. You barely glanced in my direction. It was like you didn't even see me."

"I saw you. You were wearing black jeans and a gray Henley. You hung out in the kitchen by the keg most of the night, watching the beer pong tournament."

"You kept your back to me, and I couldn't keep my eyes off your ass every time you bent forward to take your shot. When Spence and I played you and Sam, it was hard to concentrate because I kept imagining what you looked like under your dress. I knew you weren't wearing a bra, but I wanted to know if your panties matched your dress. Were they black? Would they sparkle in the light?"

His voice fades away as I replay that night in my mind. Sam and I kicking ass at beer pong. Her getting so drunk she passed out early. Spencer and Mia saying good-bye before the ball dropped, leaving me and Jay alone with only a handful of people that hadn't passed out.

The words Spencer whispered in my ear as he held me tight, wishing me a happy new year.

A new year, a new chance. The slate's been wiped clean. Make the most of it, Beauty Queen.

I remember laughing at him because he rhymed and called me Beauty Queen. He was fairly drunk when they left but Mia was coherent. Her words didn't have the impact Spencer's seemed to.

It's time to start living and stop hiding, Andi.

Looking back now, they should have. Her message was perfectly clear. They all knew what we were hiding. We weren't fooling anyone, except ourselves. Which means Sam probably knew and never said anything.

"They all knew, didn't they?" I ask, turning my head so I can look in his eyes as he answers.

"I think so."

"Even Sam?"

Jay flinches but his smile never wavers. "If she did, she was in denial as much as we were. Sam loved me and I loved her," he continues, his stare penetrating me as he speaks. The jealousy I expect to feel never surfaces. "She was a fighter and wasn't ready to give up on us even though I think we both knew we weren't meant to last. We didn't talk about our future. Not once in the two years we were together."

"Why wouldn't she say something? Why wouldn't she confront us? It's not like she was afraid of confrontation." If anything, Sam was less filtered than any of us. She spoke her mind. You never had to guess what she was thinking or how she felt. Which makes me wonder why, if she knew there was something more between Jay and I, she never mentioned it. To anyone.

"I think she was afraid to be alone. We were all getting ready to graduate, to leave town, and she had one more year of school. If she thought she was going to lose you in a few months anyway, she would have wanted to cherish the time she had left with you."

"And you," I quickly add, averting my eyes and focusing on the mess that is my suitcase. Clothes are hanging over the edge. There are a few random pieces strewn around the room from where Jay's tossed them in his haste to get me naked. "Why would she hold onto you?"

"I don't know. Maybe it was her way of holding on to all of us. If she let me go, I would have run to you. It was either lose us both or keep silent and things don't change."

Little memories flash through my mind. Things that seemed insignificant at the time but now are like blinking neon signs.

"The camping trip," I whisper.

"The summer before senior year? What about it?"

"She didn't want to go. She was trying to get out of it."

"And?" he asks, not following my train of thought.

"She pushed me to go and tried to back out at the last second. It would have been me and you and Spencer and Mia. Instead of having a fifth wheel, it would have been two pairs. If I hadn't forced Sam to go ..." I let my voice trail off.

"She was setting us up. She wanted to see what would happen if we were left alone, without her around."

"Yeah. She tried to back out of the weekend we spent at the lake that summer, too. And our trip to Nashville."

The argument I had with Sam the night before we left for Nashville is suddenly fresh in my mind.

"JUST GO WITHOUT ME. I'M NOT REALLY FEELING IT."

"It was your idea," I practically scream as I zip up my overnight bag.

"I hate the city. I don't know what I was thinking." She's avoiding eye contact, fingering the pages of the latest romance novel I picked up at the bookstore that afternoon.

"If you're not going, I'm not either. I only agreed because you insisted I come with you guys. I'm the odd man out as it is."

"If I'm not there you won't be."

"If you're not there, I have no reason to go. Don't get me wrong, I love our friends, but you're the only reason I know them. You're the glue, Sam. My sister from another mister. If you're not feeling this trip, fine. I'll stay here with you. We'll binge watch Gilmore Girls *from the beginning and eat junk food all weekend."*

It's more of a trick than anything. Sam is the only person I've ever met that isn't a fan of Gilmore Girls. *Being from a small town, the show doesn't appeal to her, I guess.*

Sam smiles but it doesn't reach her eyes. I can tell she's not happy about going but she's relenting so I don't give it a second thought. "Fine. We can go."

———

VIVID IMAGES OF JAY TRYING ON COWBOY HATS BRINGS A smile to my face. He notices, turns me in his arms, and gently presses hip lips to mine.

"Remembering all the fun we had that night?" he asks when he pulls away.

"Actually, I was thinking about how silly you looked in all the cowboy hats you insisted on trying."

Jay's bark of laughter startles me, causing me to jump back, tripping over my own two feet, sending me flailing toward the cold, wood floors. I'm not surprised when he catches me before I land, pulling me up and into his arms.

"I've got you."

"That seems to be something you say a lot."

"Well, if you'd stop trying to kiss the ground," he jokes, kissing my forehead before moving lower to my nose, and finally the place I want him most, my lips.

Putting every emotion I have into that kiss, I try and show Jay how I feel about him since I'm unable to say the words aloud, too scared to confess everything. I shouldn't be. He's already said he loves me. For some reason admitting it to him, to myself, that I feel the same, scares me more than losing him by remaining silent.

"We should probably get going," he mumbles against my lips before capturing my reply.

Spencer and Mia are probably waiting for us.

Wondering why we ran out earlier. Spencer has texted Jay no less than half a dozen times asking for information. Wanting to know what we've pieced together.

Pressing my palms against his chest, his heart beats out a steady rhythm beneath my hands as I push him away. The loss of his lips against mine is heartbreaking but necessary. I could live the rest of my life happily if he kept kissing me. *Who needs food or water when you have love?*

As the thought crosses my mind, my stomach rumbles.

"I guess we should probably feed you, too," Jay says with a laugh.

"Yeah. I could go for some bar food. The greasier the better."

After quickly fixing my hair and applying the red lipstick I bought before leaving LA in honor of Sam, Jay and I are out the door in five minutes and walking hand in hand through the old, wooden doors of Riley's Pub ten minutes later. Mia and Spence are seated at a table in the corner, laughing with a few familiar faces when we finally spot them through the crowd.

As we approach a tingling sensation washes over me. The closer we get, the stronger the feeling is. Giving Jay's hand an accidental squeeze when I shiver, he pulls me to a stop and gives me a questioning look.

"He's here. I know it. I can feel it," I explain, leaning in close so I don't have to holler over the loud music and conversations happening around us.

The place is packed. There are people standing shoulder to shoulder at the bar. Mindi looks like she's ready to pull her hair out every time someone hollers her name, and the waitresses are sprinting back and forth from the bar to tables.

I worked here for two years and it was never this busy. Not once.

This is for Sam.

And it appears the entire town has shown up to show their support.

Every face seems familiar. Every voice bringing back forgotten memories. I can still remember what most of them would order to drink. Who tipped well. Who was stingy. Who to keep an arm's length from after a few drinks.

"We knew he would be, Drea. Just breathe. Tomorrow, this ends."

Which should make me happy. Because we know he's on our list. We know the police will put the final pieces of the puzzle together. Which means tomorrow is also the day I have to say good-bye to Mia, Spencer, and Jay. Tomorrow I go back to LA. To a job that's brought me comfort in the years since losing Sam, but I have a feeling will now be a constant reminder of her death. A reminder that there are bad people in the world. Some that stand out and others that blend into the crowd. People you would never suspect to be dark and dangerous are lurking among us all the time.

Like right now.

In this very bar.

Somewhere in the crowd, is a killer.

A man who stole the life of my best friend.

Who wanted someone so he took her. And when she didn't want him back, killed her.

"Tomorrow can't come soon enough," I mutter, though I'm certain he can't hear me as I turn my back to him and walk to where our friends are still laughing without a care in the world.

All laughter comes to a halt when I silently slip onto the empty stool, Jay sliding up behind me and wrapping his arms around my shoulders.

Spencer and I share a knowing look.

One that says *I'm ready.*

We're ready.

We've figured it out. The missing piece.

And I pray it's enough to finally put this to bed. Enough for justice to reign true.

All he does is nod, returning his attention to Brandon and Ruth Royal.

"Are you enjoying your stay?" I hear Brandon ask. When I look away from Spence, I notice his attention is now focused on me.

"Yes. I love what you've done with the place. How long ago did you remodel?" I ask, attempting to make conversation even though I'd rather not.

"Gosh, it's been about what? Five years? Six?" he asks, his question directed at Ruth.

"Something like that. Those few months are kind of a blur. Every time someone picks up a hammer, I have flashbacks of you and Ben fixing up the place." Ruth shudders at the thought even though she's giggling. "I'm just glad it's over."

"Well, you did a great job," Jay pipes up. "Really. It's the nicest place to stay in town."

"I appreciate that," Brandon says, offering Jay his hand.

Mia changes the topic to Ruth's amazing culinary skills, reminding me how hungry I am. Jay waves over a waitress, orders us a few drinks and some food. As she rushes off in a frenzy, he picks me up, steals my seat, and places me in his lap. His movements don't go unnoticed by anyone at our table, all eyes falling to us.

When I chance a glance in Mia's direction a few minutes later, she's grinning at me from ear to ear. All I do is shrug my shoulders and smile back at her. There's no hiding it at this point.

Things will change again in less than twenty-four hours.

I have no idea what happens next, so I'm going to live in the moment and being close to Jay is exactly where I want to be. It's where I was meant to be.

nineteen

WHEN MINDI TAKES THE STAGE AND TAPS THE MIC, silence descends around us. She's been known to steal the show a time or two when jumping on stage to sing karaoke but tonight isn't about her belting out a classic Reba song or shaking her ass to the latest pop fad.

It's all about Sam.

And as much as I've held it together for the past two days as I've listened to person after person talk about what Sam meant to them and how she touched their lives, I have a feeling Mindi's words are going to bring me to tears.

Jay must know as well because he tightens his hold on me.

"First off, thank you all for being here tonight. I've known most of you since I moved to Great Falls twenty years ago. This wasn't my destination of choice. I was planning on stopping for the night and moving on the next day. My car had other ideas, and I've been here ever since, helping you drown your sorrows with our friends Jose and Jack."

The crowd laughs even though I suspect Mindi's statement is true.

"I have had the pleasure to watch so many of you grow up into upstanding members of the community. You've worked your way through college, started businesses of your own, taken over for your parents, and been loyal patrons of Riley's for years. Sam was no different. She was only four or five years old when I first met her. I'd just rolled into town and needed a pick me up. Imagine my surprise when I walked into the Java Bean and was greeted by a child standing on a step stool behind the counter, taking orders for her mama.

"Her energy and zest for life was obvious even back then. She was animated and excited to help. Her smile lit up the room, but it was her large, brown, doe eyes that captured my attention. For a little girl, she saw more than she should have. She asked me if I was okay and sounded genuinely concerned. When I told her my car was giving me problems, she told me it was a sign I was meant to be here. That Great Falls was my new home."

Mindi pauses and looks out over the crowd. Someone close to her waves a tissue over their head, and she takes it, dabbing at her eyes.

"I told myself I wasn't going to cry but I should have known." The crowd chuckles. The only time I've ever seen her cry is when she's angry. I was warned my first day to run the other direction if her tears ever made their presence known. "I had the pleasure of watching that beautiful young girl grow into a woman, face every challenge in life head on, and do it with her chin lifted in defiance. Nothing was going to bring her down. Bumps in the road only made her stronger.

"Honestly, I believe she had the right attitude about that. Because every time she stumbled, she stood back up, determination in her eye. Every time life tried to push her down, she pushed back. She was a fighter, a warrior, stronger than any other woman I've ever met. I was proud to call her my friend. I'm proud to have known her. To have been close to such a vibrant, young woman who had big goals in life I have no doubt she would have achieved. But she didn't share those goals with you. I was her confidant and kept her secrets. Until today. I think she would have wanted you all to know where she would be today if she had been given the chance."

Mindi pulls a well-worn piece of paper from her apron and slowly unfolds it.

"Sam wrote this a few days before she died. All her friends were graduating, and she knew her last year of college meant making life-changing decisions. These were her dreams. Her goals. What she was planning to accomplish after graduation." She reads over the list before clearing her throat and sharing Sam's words with us. "To find a man that loves me and only me. For who I am and who I want to be. To teach at Great Falls Elementary and inspire young minds to be themselves. To one day take over the Java Bean so my mom can relax for the first time in her life. To travel the World: California, New York, Paris, and Italy first."

Mindi keeps reading but I zone out. Sam never shared any of this with me. When I would ask her about what she wanted to do with her life, she'd say teach. Anytime we talked about traveling the world, she said she'd go wherever as long as the adventure was epic.

Her life still seemed up in the air most of the time, as if she was afraid to make plans. To make decisions.

From the way Mindi makes it sound, she started making plans while we were all gone on vacation. When she was here alone. Because she knew in only a few short months, she would be on her own.

Of all the things on her list, the one that sticks out the most to me is the first.

To find a man that loves me and only me.

No interpretation necessary. She knew how Jay felt about me.

"Lastly," Mindi says, her voice cutting through the guilt that's slowly beginning to settle in the pit of my stomach, "she wanted to have a family. Sam loved kids and she wanted an entire soccer team. She wanted to show them the love she had felt her entire life. From this community. From her friends and family. Mostly, from her mother. Summer may have raised Sam by herself, but she didn't do it alone. We all had a hand in raising her. We all kept our eyes on her when Summer wasn't around.

"She impacted each and every one of our lives. Her smile brightened even the darkest of days. Her spirit was contagious. And I'll be honest with you," Mindi states, her voice suddenly less upbeat, "I feel like we let her down. We failed Sam. The one time she needed us most and we weren't there. I feel personally responsible for her death and so should each of you."

Shit!

This is not good. Angry Mindi is rearing her ugly head and there's no telling what will happen next.

"And what's worse, no one wants to accept responsibility for their actions. Whoever you are, you're hiding in shame. Because this entire town deserves an apology. Summer deserves an apology, and Sam deserves to rest in peace. So, if you're in this room, as I suspect you are, show yourself, you fucking coward."

Okay, someone needs to take the microphone away from her. This is only going to get worse.

"Let this town rest. Step forward and be accountable!" Tears are freely flowing down Mindi's face as she screams, the microphone no longer necessary to hear her, her voice laced with pain and sorrow. I can only imagine she's kept those very feelings pent up like I have and now the dam has broken.

The room is silent as heads turn left and right, scanning the crowd as they wait for someone to confess their sins. It doesn't happen, and Mindi eventually steps off the stage, the music comes back to life, but the energy in the room has changed.

"That was hard to watch," Mia says, sliding off her stool. "I'm going to go check on her."

Nodding in agreement, I silently follow Mia across the bar to the kitchen entrance. When we push through the doors, two cooks and a waitress, eyes wide with fear, point toward the back door.

"I thought you quit," I state, placing my hands on my hips as I stand in front of Mindi.

She's sitting on the cold concrete, resting her head back against the building, cigarette in one hand and a bottle of Jack in the other.

"I'm not smoking," she snorts, flicking the cigarette, causing the ash to fall.

"Then what are you doing out here?" Mia asks, stepping up next to me.

"What's it look like?"

Mindi's a hard-ass. She doesn't talk about her feelings. She's normally the one offering her shoulder to cry on, but right now, the roles need to be reversed, as much as she's going to hate it.

"It looks like my friend is in desperate need of a hug. It looks like the strongest woman I know is falling apart with good reason. It looks like ..." I pause and wait for her to lift her eyes to mine before I continue. When she doesn't, I kneel down to her eye level and lift her chin. "It looks like you're hurting as much as the rest of us, maybe more, because you've kept these feelings bottle up for five years."

"I should have been here that night," she whispers, tears glistening in her eyes.

"We all wish we'd been here that night. We all feel responsible because we loved her. It doesn't change what happened, and blaming yourself won't bring her back." Keeping my eyes trained on hers, I try and alleviate the pain, even just a little. "We will find him, Mindi. We will get justice for Sam. I promise you that much. And when we do, you get first crack at him."

That brings a smile to her face. I can only imagine what she would do to him if left alone in a room without a camera. I doubt he'd be able to walk after she was done with him.

Taking the cigarette from between her fingers as I stand, I drop it to the ground, stomp it out with my foot, and extend my hand to her.

"I need a minute."

"Take all the time you need. I'll jump behind the bar and fill in until you get back," I say, repressing my smile.

"The hell you will," she roars as she pushes herself off the ground and takes a swig of Jack. "You don't even know how to properly mix your own drinks."

She doesn't resist when I pull her into my arms. Or when Mia wraps her arms around both of us. We stand like that for a few minutes before walking back into the bar as silently as we left it.

The place has emptied out a little, more than likely because of the absence of the bartender. Or maybe people were trying to avoid the rage they expected to see on her face when she returned.

"All good?" Spence asks as Mia and I approach.

"No, but good enough for now," is all Mia says as she steps between his legs and wraps herself around him.

Spencer holds her tight, his eyes focused on me. I watch them in awe. Their love is as strong as I've ever seen. They survived the worst of the storm. They've fought to stay together, to stay here, to face Sam's death head on. To find justice when it appeared all hope had been lost.

"We'll get him," I say to Spence after a few beats.

"I know, Andi. The alternative isn't an option anymore. I need this. You need this. Most of all, the town needs it."

All I can do is nod as Jay reaches for me, pulling me to his side and wrapping his arm around my shoulder. Pressing his lips to my temple, Jay whispers, "Are you ready to go?"

"Yeah," I say, letting out a sigh. "What time is it?"

"A little after eleven."

My body stiffens. We missed our chance. He was here. He's more than likely gone now. If he went through the park, if he visited the scene of the crime, where Sam took her last breath, we will never know. All we have to go on is the profile and my gut.

"We're gonna get going. Noon tomorrow?" Spence asks as he pulls me in for a hug.

"Yeah. We narrowed the list down to ten potential suspects. I plan to deliver the profile and then I'll hand over the list. If he's on there, you'll know right away. Listen to your gut, Spence. Trust your instinct. You know this case better than anyone."

"How confident in the profile are you?" Holding me at arm's length, Spence stares me directly in the eyes, looking for any hint of doubt.

He won't find it.

"It's spot on. Everything points in one direction, to one

person. All you have to do is put two and two together and you'll have him. I promise. I just wish I could be here when you arrest him."

"I thought you said you'd stay until he was caught?" Mia asks from next to me. When I chance a glance in her direction, she's resting her head against Jay's chest, worrying her bottom lip between her teeth. I've never seen her this insecure.

"There's no reason for me to stay at this point," I reply, my eyes leaving hers and finding Jay's. "Spence will find him. The next time you see me will be when you are walking down the aisle."

I imagine Mia rolling her eyes at my comment, but I can't pull my attention away from Jay. His eyes are dark and stormy, the deep blue specks disappearing behind the darker hue. His intentions are clear in the way his eyes are devouring me, causing my skin to prickle and desire to pool deep inside of me.

"I'm holding you to that," I hear Mia say as she wraps her arms around me.

I'm going to miss her and Spencer. It's been hard seeing them again. This entire trip was a rollercoaster ride of emotions. Still, in the end I'm glad I came. I'm happy I was able to reconnect with them. And I think Spencer was right.

Celebrating Sam's life was healing. I couldn't have done that alone. We fell apart together, and we needed to heal together.

I feel stronger than I have in years. I've smiled more in the last two days than I have the last two years.

And my heart no longer feels like it's caught in a vise grip, tightening at every turn.

"I'd like to come with you tomorrow," Jay says as he shuts the door to my room behind us.

"You're more than welcome. It's not going to take long. Twenty minutes maybe. Then I need to come back here and pack. My flight leaves at four," I explain, not wanting to think about the fact I'm leaving him in a little over twelve hours.

Unsure of when the next time I'll see him.

Knowing I love him and always have but also aware of the fact we have two completely different lives to get back to, on opposites sides of the country.

"I have to get on the road by one o'clock. How about I drive us to the station and then I'll bring you back here on my way out of town?" he suggests, pulling his shirt over his head and tossing it across the room as he's become accustom to.

Not going to lie, I like it. Not just the way he looks without a shirt on. Or his tattoo that gives him a bit of an edge I wasn't aware he had.

No, I like the way his muscles flex as he pulls his shirt off. The way they tighten when stretched over his head.

Most of all, I like the way my heart skips a beat as it happens. And the wicked smile on his face that always makes its presence known, as if he knows the dirty thoughts running through my mind and agrees with every single one of them.

"That's fine," I state, reaching out and tracing the outline of his abs with my pointer finger.

"You keep doing that and you're going to get yourself in trouble. I have other plans for us tonight," he says, taking my hand in his and pressing it flat against the center of his chest. I can feel the pounding of his heart against my palm.

"What did you have in mind?" I tease, raising an

eyebrow at him as I stare deep into his hazel eyes. They've softened since the bar, or maybe it's something else reflecting in his stare.

"I want to hold you, Drea. I want to know what it feels like when you fall asleep in my arms. I want to see the look of content on your face as my body wraps around yours."

"That's all you want?"

"For tonight, yes. More than anything, I want you to feel my love wrapped around you. Tomorrow, when we say good-bye, I don't want there to be any doubt in your mind that it's only temporary. That we were meant to be together and we'll find a way. Because I'm not giving up on us. Five years didn't change the way I felt about you, nothing ever will."

With that, Jay pulls my lips to his. His kiss is tender but passionate. When he licks the seam of my lips, I open for him. I expect his patience to wear thin as he deepens our kiss, but he remains strong as he begins to undress me.

By the time we're both in only our underwear, tucked under the covers, I'm a ball of tension and need. The moment he tucks his body against mine, a single word echoes through my mind.

Home.

twenty

WHEN I LEFT LA FOUR DAYS AGO, DREAD CONSUMED ME. I didn't want to be here. I was afraid to come back. Knowing the agony I felt five years ago would be all-consuming it was the last thing I wanted to do. Yet, I forced myself to get on the plane.

In my heart, I knew it was necessary. Not only that, but I didn't want to let Spencer down. He said he needed me here so I came.

My goal was to ignore the pain and head back home as soon as possible.

Home now has a new meaning. Home is not the place you lay your head at night, it's a feeling.

Great Falls was once my home. The people here welcomed me into their lives. My friends became my family and we navigated this crazy ride called life. Together.

As I stare at my partially packed suitcase while Jay showers, a new sense of dread is coursing through my veins.

I'm heading back to an empty apartment. No one will be there to greet me. No one to hold me at night or watch a movie with me. No one to wipe away my tears when I'm overcome with emotion.

I've always thought LA was where I was meant to be,

but life has taken on new meaning the last few days. Not just because of Jay, either.

My heart has closure.

I've accepted Sam's death.

More importantly, I've accepted the fact that I wasn't the cause of it.

Yes, I should have made my flight that morning. Yes, I should have been working that night instead of her.

At the end of the day, I screwed up, but I wasn't the one who killed her. I wasn't the reason she never made it home that night. I was only the reason she was in the park to begin with.

And I'm not the only one who made it possible for her to be in that park.

Spencer could have picked her up. Jay could have come back to town and driven her home.

We all had our reasons for not being here, for not stepping up. None of us are responsible for what happened, though.

I imagine the guilt won't dissipate any time soon. I'll always wonder what would have happened if she hadn't worked my shift but I'm no longer blaming myself.

Sam wouldn't want me to.

She'd want me to find a way to go one. To live life with a smile on my face, seeking my next adventure. She'd want my heart filled with love, not regret.

So, I will. I'll live for Sam. For the life she was cheated out of.

"You're so beautiful when you smile." Jay's words warm my heart as he wraps his arms around my waist and pulls me against his firm, damp chest. I don't care he's getting my blouse wet, or that I'm thinking about Sam. All I care about is the way I feel when I'm in his arms.

This is home.

The very definition of what it should feel like.

Warm. Welcoming. Loved.

Home is a feeling, not a place.

I repeat the phrase over and over again because home is where your heart is. And my heart belongs to Jay.

"You need to get dressed so we can head to the station," I state, turning in his arms and placing a chaste kiss over his heart. "We're going to be late."

"What if I'm not ready to leave you yet?"

"You're not leaving me," I say, taking a step back … only for him to pull me in tighter and clasp his hands behind my back.

"This suddenly feels like good-bye."

"It's not, I promise."

When I woke up in his arms this morning, I vowed it wouldn't be the last time. We still have a lot to figure out, shit to work through, distance to erase, but I will wake up in his arms again. Soon.

Jay's only response is a pantie-melting grin, his dimple making an appearance, before pressing his lips to mine for a swift kiss.

"I sure hope not," he finally says, releasing me and stepping back before dropping his towel dramatically to the floor.

If he's trying to turn me on, the kiss was plenty. Seeing him naked, taking in all of him, every glorious angle, only heightens the growing need I'm feeling.

But we don't have time for that right now. We really are running late. Not to mention, I want my last memory of him to be pure.

There will be plenty of time to make more memories. Dirty, clean, and every kind in between.

With his bag slung over his shoulder, Jay leads me out the front door of the B&B and to his waiting car. The drive to the police station is short and quiet. There's not a whole lot we can say about what happens next. Everything is riding on the profile I'm about to present and I need to stay focused.

When we arrive, the chief and his entire force are waiting for us. Being a small town, there are only a handful of cops, including Spencer. They're seated around a conference room table, eagerly awaiting my presentation.

Jay stands in the back of the room, between Spencer and the chief, who seems to be in a foul mood this morning. With a nod of encouragement, I launch into my speech.

"Good morning. For those of you who don't know me, my name is Andrea Morris. I graduated from GFU five years ago and Samantha Bridges was my best friend. With a degree in psychology and behavioral sciences, I've been working as a profiler for the state of California for the last four years. Today, I would like to present you with a profile of the man who murdered Sam with the sincere hope that we're able to find justice for her, her family, and her friends."

The eight men and two women sitting around the table all nod at me in unison. I can see the determination in their eyes. They want this as much as I do.

"Please remember that a profile is not a hundred percent accurate. Every murderer is different. From their motives to mental state. Someone you may never expect could be a cold-blooded killer. He knows how to only show you what you want to see. To hide his true self. That's something I think this particular person has done. He's mastered the art of deception.

"Yes, we are looking for a man. More than likely he was in his mid-to-late twenties at the time of the murder. And you know him. He is a local of the Great Falls community. He knew Sam. Whether he came here for school or grew up here, he's part of this town. To better understand who you might be looking for, I need to explain who he is inside first. The person you don't see.

"There are two kinds of killers … organized and unorganized. This man is organized. He planned to kill Sam. He took the necessary steps to avoid being caught. There wasn't a detail he didn't go over. From wearing black clothes head-to-toe to wearing gloves so there was no DNA evidence. He bought the rope and tape in advance, more than likely from another town, and he paid in cash so his purchase couldn't be traced back to him. He's also what I'd categorize as a pathological, obsessive killer.

"What that means is he watches, stalks his victims. He knew Sam's habits. Knew she walked home through the park. Knew her schedule and was a regular at Riley's. Over time, he became obsessed with her. He would have tried to be her friend first, and in his mind, their relationship was blossoming. He would have asked her out on multiple occasions. Sam was involved with someone else and would have turned down his advances. This would have angered him. It was the trigger for his rage."

Pausing to make sure I'm not speaking too fast, I tuck a stray piece of hair behind my ear and glance around the room. The officers are scribbling notes, completely engaged in what I'm saying.

"This man suffers from PTSD, more than likely from abuse as a child at the hands of his father or male role model. It could have been physical, but more often than not it's verbal. He was made to feel like he wasn't good enough, no matter how hard he tried. He may have excelled at some things, but not all. If he was great at school, he did poor with athletics, or vice versa. His father was critical of his inabilities and compared him to others, making him feel worthless. His mother, on the other hand, was his savior.

"As resentful as he is toward his father, he has a great relationship with his mother. He compares every woman to her and has a hard time maintaining a healthy relationship because of this. Sam fit into the tiny mold. In his mind, she was the perfect woman for him, and her rejection was the catalyst for his rage. It was a murder of passion. His intention was to kill her because, in his mind, if he couldn't have her, no one should be able to have her.

"He did make two mistakes, though, and this is how you'll eventually be able to convict him once you determine who he is. At some point in time, he inserted himself into the investigation. He needed to know what you knew. He made himself available to help in any way possible. You more than likely interviewed him and then dismissed him as a suspect."

"We talked to half the town," an older, pudgy officer states. He looks seasoned, his uniform a lighter shade of navy than the officer next to him. He may have worked the original case.

"I know, and I have a list of potential suspects for you to consider. People who I highly recommend you interview a second time. In his initial interview he would have been relaxed. His arrogance wouldn't have been noticed, but I guarantee he was smiling without a care in the world while you spoke with him. Because he knew you weren't onto him. He was going to get away with it and the cocky grin on his face said it all. But you didn't know it at the time.

"When you interview him again, he'll be nervous. The entire town is aware the case is still open, that it's being looked at again. The ones with a clear conscience won't panic but he will."

"What else did we miss?" the same officer asks, blowing out a breath of frustration.

"He left no evidence, but he did take some with him. Sam's apron wasn't with her body. It wasn't noted in any of the files, but she would have had it with her. It's his trophy. Yes, he'll go back to the scene to relive his crime, but because he's local, you'd never think twice about him being there. He took her apron and has it stashed somewhere. He'll want to touch it, smell it. Holding it in his hands will bring him great joy."

"Sick bastard," I hear someone mutter.

"That's the thing, he is sick but he's also completely normal. He's the life of the party. Everyone's friend. Good looking. He fits in with the crowd, but he also knows how to blend in when necessary. One minute he'll be there and the next he's gone. You'd never suspect him because he's constantly around, always pleasant and smiling. He masks his pain and it festers on the inside. Like I said, Sam hurt his feelings and it caused him to snap. He waited until the perfect moment and then struck. There was no advanced warning. No signs anyone missed. If she hadn't been in the park that night, he would have gotten to her another time. He planned everything out in advance and watched and waited for his moment. It just so happened to be that night."

"And what do you expect us to do with this information?" This is from the chief. Who's standing with his arms crossed, a sour expression on his face.

"I promised you I'd give you a complete profile of the

person who murdered Sam. I have. I can't force you to do anything with it, but I highly recommend having a fresh set of eyes look over the case, keeping the profile in mind. Perhaps they'll see something no one else does. Maybe someone will stand out to them. Because I guarantee you spoke with him five years ago. He's in the files. He made his presence known and he's out there, still watching this department. Especially right now."

Spencer and Jay both nod at me in approval. I wasn't about to let the chief walk all over me after all the time and hard work I put into this profile. With Jay's help, it came together quicker and more complete than I expected it to. I wouldn't have been able to finish it without him.

Normally, bouncing ideas off another person would only distract me. Especially when that other person has abs that look like Jay's. All cut and firm—

"You said you have a list?" one of the female officers asks.

"I do, but before I share it with you, I want you to consider every member of the community. Based on what I've shared with you today about him, is there anyone that stands out? Anyone your guts tells you to bring in and talk to? If so, jot those names down. Hold onto them. They might match someone on the list. Your best lead will always come from what your instincts tell you. If it's Joe Schmo that always gets hammered at the bar on Tuesday nights, you'll know. It won't be someone that you have run-ins with for police business, though. He's clean. If he has a record, it would be for minor things. Traffic violations. Parking tickets. Fights. There is nothing about this man that screams killer. He hides it well."

"And when we find him?" Spencer asks.

"When you find him, you'll need to find Sam's apron so

you can convict him. You can't put the murder weapon in his hand. You can't prove he's guilty without DNA evidence. You'll have to find the missing piece to pin it on him or you'll have to let him walk away. I know that's not something any of you want to do. You don't want a murderer in your town. You don't want to have to worry about your wives and daughters. You want him behind bars where he deserves to be. You want to make Great Falls feel safe again. That won't happen until you catch him."

"You make it sound so simple," the older cops states flippantly.

"Clear your mind of everything you know. Focus only on what I've told you today. Don't think about the case, think about the man."

"It could be a handful of people."

"I can think of at least three."

"I have five names on my list."

Everyone starts to speak at once, arguing over the possibilities of who it could be. It's not until the chief clears his throat that all talking ceases.

"One last thing before I leave you with the profile," I say, waving around the information I've printed out for them. A bulleted list of characteristics. "He will fit ninety-nine percent of what's on here. Narrow your list down and then bring them in for questioning. You will know right away who it is. Then, find Sam's apron and nail the bastard. It won't be at his home or place of business. It'll be stashed somewhere in town. Somewhere he visits often. A close friend or family member's house. Hidden out of sight but easily accessible.

"Sam deserves justice. This town deserves to sleep with their doors unlocked again. Good luck, and if I can be of any further assistance, please don't hesitate to reach out.

Both the chief and Detective Crawford know how to reach me. Thank you."

Every officer shakes my hand, thanking me for my help. As they leave the room one by one, Jay, Spence, and the chief approach. I pull the piece of notebook paper out of my back pocket and hand it to Spencer.

"He's on this list. Let them narrow it down to only a few people before you show it to them," I say, my voice sounding authoritative, Spencer's lips curling to keep from laughing.

"Will do," he answers with a salute before pulling me in for a hug so tight I expel all the breath in my lungs. "I'll keep you posted and talk to you in a few days, okay?"

"Sounds good."

"Thank you for taking the time," the chief begins, surprising me. "I won't deny I was skeptical, but after hearing what you had to say, I have a few ideas of who may be behind Sam's death myself. I'll be curious to see if any of them are on your list."

"Listen to your gut. You've been doing this long enough. Instinct is a funny thing. If you have perspective, it'll never steer you wrong. I hope I was able to shed some light on the case today."

"You did. Thank you very much, Miss Morris."

After shaking the chief's hand, he steps passed me but not before clapping both Spencer and Jay on the shoulders before leaving the three of us alone.

"We should get going," I start, pulling Spence in for another hug, not ready to say good-bye yet.

"We?" he questions. "Something y'all want to tell me before you ride off into the sunset together?"

"We're not riding off together," I say, smacking him on

the chest as I pull away. "We rode together. Jay has to get on the road, and I have a plane to catch."

"If that's your story," he notes with a wicked grin as he man-hugs Jay and winks at me.

For now, that's the only story there is to tell. My hope is that the next time I see Spencer, the story will have developed a bit more. The beginning is solid. The middle was rocky. But the ending ... that's what I'm most interested in reading.

twenty-one

AFTER MAKING A PIT STOP AT BLUSH TO SAY GOOD-BYE TO Mia, and another stop at the Java Bean to see Summer, Jay and I head back to the Hideaway to say our own goodbyes.

We've been standing outside for ten minutes. Neither of us have said a word as Jay holds me close. His woodsy smell and the feel of his beating heart beneath my cheek are all I can focus on as I find the courage to push him away. He needs to get on the road, and with each passing minute it becomes harder to say good-bye.

A door slams behind me, breaking the bubble we'd put ourselves in.

When I push away, I see uncertainty in Jay's eyes. It reflects the way I feel in my heart.

"I'll call you as soon as my plane lands," I state, averting my eyes to the cracked sidewalk beneath my feet.

"You were amazing in there. You gave them everything they need to find this guy."

"Thanks." My voice is barely audible as the single word catches in my throat.

"Drea," Jay whispers, lifting my chin with his finger. "This is not good-bye."

"It feels like it."

"We survived five years apart. Years where we could have used each other to lean on. That time allowed us to grow as individuals, to figure out who we are and what we want from life. For me, it solidified the fact that I love you, I want to be with you. There is no one else on this Earth who will ever compare to you. You're it for me. One day, you'll see that everything I did, everything I sacrificed, it was all for you. So we could be together. Today. Tomorrow. Next year. You are my forever," he finishes, cupping my face with his hands and sealing his words with a kiss.

"Forever," I whisper when he finally pulls away and rests his forehead against mine. "That's a hell of a long time to put up with you. I'm not sure if I'm up for the challenge or not."

"I think you might be the only one who can handle what I have to give. My heart beats for yours."

"You own my soul," I state. It's the only way I can explain how I feel about him.

"Good. Because you own mine."

With that, Jay kisses me one last time before getting in his car and driving off. No good-bye. No, I'll see you later.

All I can do is stand in the middle of the sidewalk and watch him drive off with my heart in tow.

Long after he's out of sight, I force myself to walk the four steps up the porch of the Hideaway and open the front door. The staircase proves to be a bigger challenge to navigate as my legs feel heavy, knowing I'm going to be putting even more distance between us as soon as I get on the plane.

Distance I want to erase.

There is nowhere in this world I want to be other than by Jay's side.

I've always known it but been too afraid to admit it and terrified to act on it. Even now, the thought scares me, but it also makes me smile.

After torturing myself for years, allowing the guilt to consume me, I'd like to think Sam would be happy for us as well. That two people she loved most in this world, love each other. That we've found our happiness. Someone to accept us the way we are.

And if she's watching over us, I hope she can see how sorry we both are for betraying her. It was not something we meant to do. Not something we were proud of.

There are moments in life that define you. People that help you figure out who you are and who you want to be.

Meeting Jay opened my eyes to love.

Being friends with Sam sparked my drive for adventure.

Spencer warmed my heart with laughter.

Mia kept us all grounded.

Summer made me feel accepted.

Mindi nurtured my wounded soul.

The people I've met, the memories we've made, will always be a part of who I am. A part of the woman I've grown to become. They've helped mold me into a strong, vibrant woman.

Even Sam's death has made me stronger. I'm a survivor.

But this weekend changed me more than any of the years I spent here. It healed a part of me that's been broken.

The reason acceptance is the hardest step is because it's final. Once you really, truly accept someone is gone, the pain becomes real. You don't have another chance to tell them you love them. To show them you care.

In your mind, you didn't do it enough when they were alive.

The truth is, if you truly love someone, you don't have to say the words. Your actions will always be enough.

Sam knew I loved her. She knew she was my best

friend. I told her often, but I didn't have to. My actions spoke loud enough.

And vice versa.

I will never question how much she cared about me. How much our friendship meant to her. It was everything.

Which is why it made having feelings for Jay that much harder. I wasn't willing to lose her for a chance with him. In a sense, I cared more about her than I did my own happiness. More than I cared about Jay.

And that's okay.

Sam deserved our love.

No matter how we feel about each other, no matter what happens in the future, Sam will always have our love. Mine and Jay's. Because you don't stop loving someone after they're gone. You just love silently.

————

I'M ZIPPING UP MY SUITCASE, SCANNING THE ROOM TO MAKE sure I have everything, when my phone rings.

"Spence," I say, drawing his name out. The hairs on my arms are standing on end. There's only one reason he would be calling.

"Are you still in town?" His words are rushed and he sounds out of breath.

"Yeah. I just finished packing. I'm about to leave. Why?"

"Stay there. I may need your help."

"Spencer—" I start, but the line goes dead.

Pulling my suitcase off the folding stand, I hear something hit the floor and immediately begin searching the area. Out of the corner of my eye I spot a screw by the leg of the stand, and after setting my suitcase aside, I pick it up to inspect it.

The drive has been stripped and the treads are practically bare. It's obvious the screw has been worn down over the years. It's small, barely an inch in length, and rusted.

Spencer bursts through my door at the same moment I notice the return air vent is hanging lose.

"We know who it is," he says after slamming the door behind him.

"That's great, Spence," I reply excitedly as I attempt to put the screw back into place with only my fingertips. "Is he in custody?"

"The chief is on his way to pick him up right now. I wanted to tell you in person. Where's Jay?"

"He already left," I reply, pressing my hand against the vent as I continue to fidget with the screw, causing the one on the left to wiggle itself lose and fall to the ground.

"Breaking things before you leave?" he asks, crouching down beside me.

"I didn't break anything. This damn screw fell out and I was trying to put it back in and the other one fell out."

"Here," Spence says, picking up the fallen screw and nudging me out of the way. "Let me try."

Securing the vent to the wall with his hand the way I was, Spencer attempts to put both screws back in place. Once one is seated, he moves to the other, causing the first to fall back out.

"They're stripped. Just let Brandon know and he'll get new ones. They cost a buck, if that."

Releasing the vent, he gently lowers it to the floor and stands to his full height, setting the screws on the dresser. I'm frozen in place as my eyes fall on what lays hidden behind the old piece of metal.

"Spence," I mumble, his name barely slipping passed my

lips as shock knocks me on my ass. Literally. I fall backward, landing with a thud.

"Are you okay?"

I point toward the vent, and Spencer laughs. "Do dark places scare you now? You were the one that loved to go to the haunted houses, Andi. The one that always dragged Sam, knowing she was going to scream every time she rounded a corner. I swear—"

"Spencer!" I holler, interrupting his trip down memory lane. "I'm not scared of dark holes. There's something in there."

Crouching back down, Spencer tries to see what's in the hole, but his head blocks the light. Pulling his cell phone from his back pocket, he turns on his flashlight and shines it inside, the sight causing him to take a seat next to me.

We sit in silence, neither of us sure what we can say in this moment. Spencer's flashlight is still pointed at Sam's apron, a multicolored, fuzzy pen sticking out of one of the folds.

"You were going to arrest someone without the evidence I told you we needed?" I finally ask.

"The chief was convinced it was him. He didn't want to wait. There's a judge issuing a search warrant for multiple properties right now. This place included."

"I can't believe Brandon would do this," I say, the words slipping passed my lips as I expel a loud breath.

"He didn't. It was his brother, Ben."

"Ben Royal?"

"Yeah. Every single one of the officers wrote his name down while you were presenting the profile. Every. Single. One. They all went to school with the Royals. They know him. Knew he had a bad relationship with his father. He was a track star in high school but a fuck up in all other aspects. And he likes to be the center of attention.

"Even the chief was sure it was him. Before we looked at your list. Before we watched his interview from five years ago. He wasn't called in by anyone, he came in and offered to help. Claimed he walked through the park that night on his way to Riley's and saw Sam walking home. Waved at her but didn't stop to talk to her."

"That wasn't in the file."

"It appears there was a lot missing from the investigation. Things they didn't think were important were left out of the notes. The chief's job is on the line. I think that's why he wanted this case closed. He had to know if anyone found out how badly they fucked up the initial investigation, heads would roll. Mainly his."

Spencer finally turns off his flashlight and tosses his phone on the floor next to us.

"Don't you need to call this in?" I ask, my eyes still focused on the now dark hole. I don't need light to have a clear image of what I know is there.

"Yeah. I just need a minute to process, ya know? It's over, Andi. It's finally over." Spencer let's out a gruff breath, and when I turn to thank him for his hard work and dedication, I find tears streaming down his cheeks.

Wrapping my arm around his broad shoulder, I pull him to me, and he lays down with his head in my lap.

"Thank you," he mutters, wiping away the tears.

"None of this would have been possible without you, Spence. You dedicated your life to solving Sam's murder. You never gave up. Not even when it all seemed hopeless. Not when life got hard. Not when you wanted to run. You stayed and you made sure someone was always searching for answers.

"I may have put together the picture of who did it, but you kept hope alive. You brought the town together to celebrate Sam's life. And now you get to tell everyone that the case is closed. Not because it's been five years and it's time, but because you caught the bastard responsible."

"I really should call this in."

"Take another minute to relish in the victory. To let closure wash over you, Spence. Remember this feeling for the rest of your life. Once you make that call, this place is going to be a flurry of activity."

Spence closes his eyes and breathes deeply. Reaching for my phone, I quickly shoot off a text to Jay. I know he's on his way home, that he probably won't get the message for hours, but he deserves to know it's over. He deserves to know the name of the man that took Sam's life.

Me: Case closed. They're arresting Ben Royal right now for Sam's murder.

This isn't just closure for Spencer, it's for all of us.

My phone rings seconds after I send the message.

"Hey," I say, keeping my voice low even though Spencer is now staring up at me from where his head is still resting in my lap.

"Are you serious?" The sound of relief in Jay's voice mixed with disbelief causes an ache in my chest to build.

I can feel the pieces of my heart being put back together.

"Yes, Jay. The chief is on his way to arrest him, and coincidentally, Spencer and I stumbled on Sam's apron."

"What?" You can hear the shock in Jay's voice. "Where? How? I don't understand. That happened so fast. It's barely been two hours since you presented the profile."

After relaying to Jay everything Spencer explained to me, I hang up with the promise to keep him updated on the situation. Spencer finally calls the chief and informs him of what we found.

It'll be an hour before the crime scene unit arrives, so Spencer and I are babysitting the evidence. No one is allowed in the room with us. There's an officer standing guard outside of the open door, and another in the room watching to make sure we don't contaminate the evidence.

"So," I start, wanting to talk about anything other than why we're stuck in this room. Why I'm going to miss my plane back home. "When are you going to propose to Mia?"

"I figure I'll let things die down a little, make her squirm for a few weeks, and then surprise her. Why? You got a better idea?"

"Actually I do, but you have to keep an open mind," I say, echoing the words he spoke to me a week ago when he called to ask me to come here.

"That's my line."

"I stole it," I counter quickly.

"I don't like it. You know I can't refuse your requests. I'm a sucker for my ladies."

Rolling my eyes, I'm about to launch into detail about my big idea when there's a commotion outside of the door. I hear hollering, recognizing the voice immediately.

"This is my house. You have no right to be here," Brandon yells. "I don't give a shit if you have a warrant. This is my business. I've done nothing wrong." There's a long pause before footsteps grow louder as they climb.

"Chief," the officer at the door says as he steps aside.

"Well, that didn't go well," he says in lieu of a greeting. "Though, I can't blame the guy. I'd be pissed if my brother killed someone and hid the evidence in my house, too. Where is it?"

"In the return air vent," Spencer offers, pointing across the room but making no move to get up off the bed.

"We're not cutting corners on this. The feds are sending a crime scene unit in. They should be here any time. I want them to bag and tag the apron and all its contents. They're going to process everything at their lab. It'll be quicker than the state lab. I'm hoping to have this wrapped up by the end of the week."

"Where is he?" I hear myself ask.

"County jail. He's being held without bail. He didn't even put up a fight when we knocked on his door. Held out his hands and let us cuff him. It's like he knew we were coming for him."

He probably did, and that means he's ready to talk. To tell his side of the story. To relive the events of that night because he knows his name will be infamous in the town of Great Falls.

ONE YEAR LATER

"I NOW PRONOUNCE YOU HUSBAND AND WIFE. YOU MAY KISS the bride," the officiant announces. Jay leans in, pressing his lips to the side of my head as we watch Spencer capture Mia's lips, bending her backwards with more flare than necessary.

The small ceremony took less than a month to plan. Mainly because Spencer and I have been working together secretly behind Mia's back. The invitations were sent out the same day Mia catapulted into Spencer's arms screaming yes.

"May I present to you, for the first time, Mr. And Mrs. Spencer Crawford."

Rose petals are tossed in the air as Mia and Spencer walk hand in hand away from Sam's fountain. That's what it's come to be known as. And I can feel her here. When I'm in town, yes, but mostly here. When I come to visit and toss in a coin. When I talk to her, I do it here. The place she took her last breath.

It was only fitting to have the ceremony on sacred ground. It almost feels like Sam was a part of the celebration as the water rained down on the metal waves, sliding back into the fountain, over and over again.

The reception is just as perfect. Riley's Pub has been transformed. The normally dark and dank feel is brightened by stark white linens over the tables and sheer white drapes that hang from the ceiling, surrounded by red and blue paper lanterns, giving the space a pop of color.

"You did good," Jay says, giving my hand a squeeze.

"I didn't do it alone. Mindi was a huge help." Looking over my shoulder to where Mindi is situated behind the bar, our eyes meet, and she flashes me a bright smile.

When Spencer and I approached her on New Year's Eve about hosting the reception here, she practically jumped at the opportunity. She was already a little tipsy, the new year only minutes away, so I was surprised when I had a string of texts from her waiting for me when I woke up the next morning, complete with pictures of her vision.

The last three months have been a whirlwind of plotting and planning. Knowing Spencer was going to propose on Valentine's Day, we had to move quickly, but I couldn't be more impressed with the final product. Judging by the smile on Mia's face right now as she glides around the room, we did good.

"Spencer's a genius," Jay notes as we watch our two best friends share their first dance as husband and wife.

"Don't tell him that. His ego is big enough already," I joke as he stands, extending his hand to me.

"Think about it," he begins, leading me to the dance floor and spinning me into his arms, "he proposed on a holiday, a date he'll never forget. Then, he got married on his birthday so he'll never miss their anniversary."

Laughing as Jay spins me out and pulls me back in, I nod my head in agreement. "Yeah, I guess that was a good idea. Though I doubt he'd forget his anniversary even if today wasn't his birthday. He loves Mia and has been waiting for this moment for years."

"You think in fifty years, when his memory starts to go, he'd still be able to remember their anniversary?" he inquires as he dips me backwards, pulling me up slowly and securing me in his arms.

"When you love someone, I think you remember every moment. It's not about celebrating your love one day a year. Sure, it's a milestone, but love should be celebrated every day you wake up. Every time you kiss, you should feel their love."

Jay leans in and presses his lips to mine as he continues to lead us around the dance floor. What I assume is going to be a chaste kiss continues for far longer than anticipated, turning needier by the second. When I pull away, I can see the lust in his eyes, the deep blue specks around his hazel irises having disappeared.

Jay pulls us to a stop as the song changes. "All of Me" by John Legend begins to play, the melody drawing my attention.

This is our song.

Deemed by Jay as it was playing the night I confessed I loved him. The same night we made plans to move in together and go all in.

It's amazing how one text changed everything. Not only did it provide a sense of relief that Sam's murderer was caught, but it instilled hope in Jay.

He was halfway home already when I sent the text. He'd stopped for gas and was getting ready to call to see if I had made it to the airport when his phone buzzed in his hands.

He turned his car around and headed back here.

Straight to Summer's, where Mia, Spencer, and I were currently celebrating.

The moment I saw him standing on Summer's front porch, I knew what I wanted. It was like I could see my future perfectly. Summer must have known what I was thinking because she practically pushed me out the door and into his arms.

Her blessing meant a lot.

Sometimes I think it's what was holding me back from admitting I loved him. Not only to myself but to everyone else. Not that it wasn't clear to those around us. So, when I finally professed my love, sitting in Jay's car in from of Summer's house with "All of Me" playing on the radio, it didn't come as a surprise to anyone. Not even Jay.

Shaking my head clear of thoughts of the past, I focus on my present. My future. The man holding me in his arms as our song plays.

"You're going to get yourself in trouble if you kiss me like that again." It's a clear warning of what he's stirred deep inside of me. Last time he didn't heed it, and we ended up sneaking away from our friends at Spence and Mia's engagement party, locking the bathroom door behind us, and having a quickie on the counter.

Not that we were stealthy about it. The acoustics in the bathroom gave us away. Or it could have been the smile on Jay's face. My mused lipstick. His disheveled hair. Take your pick. Spencer and Mia were laughing at us when we rejoined the party.

"I have no idea what you're talking about," he says as he leans in only a breath away from my lips.

My eyes close as I wait for it, the kiss that's going to steal my resolve. Thoughts of another adventure behind a locked door. When it doesn't happen, I open my eyes to find Jay down on one knee.

The music has stopped, the room falling silent around us.

"I told you he was a genius. You propose on a day you'll never forget." He's smiling up at me as he pops open the lid of the tiny, black box he's holding in his hands. "I've loved you for eight years, since the moment you fell into my arms. I promise to catch you every time you stumble. To be the man you deserve. To love you unconditionally every day for the rest of your life. You own my heart and my soul. You're my home. Andrea Renee Morris, will be make me the happiest man in the world and be my wife?"

My mouth opens but no words come out. I'm utterly speechless. When I feel a nudge at my shoulder, I look to see who's standing behind me but there's no one even close.

Sam.

She's here. She's giving me the okay. Urging me to say yes.

Tears sting my eyes as I nod my head. My gaze never leaves Jay's as he slips the ring on my hand, quickly standing and pulling me into his arms. When he presses his lips to mine, I can feel every promise he just made me.

Cheers erupt around us, and when Jay finally releases me, Spencer and Mia are the first in line to congratulate us.

"Thanks, man," I hear Jay say to Spence as Mia wraps her arms around me.

"I'm so happy for you," she gleefully screeches in my ear.

"Thank you. I'm sorry he stole the show at your wedding."

Of all the places I expected Jay to propose, it wasn't

here. I've felt the slow shift in our relationship the last few weeks. I knew it was coming.

I should have. Every major step we've taken since reconnecting last year has happened fast. A month after Ben Royal was arrested, we bought a house in Great Falls and moved in together. Jay quit his government job and joined the police force here while I started a non-profit helping families cope with grief and loss.

As summer came to an end, we found out we were expecting our first child, due in only a few weeks. A little boy.

For Christmas, my parents visited Great Falls for the first time ever, thanks to Jay.

Of all the surprises over the last year, this may have been the biggest of all. We've talked about getting married. Eventually. After Sammy, our little boy, is born. When I can walk down the aisle without waddling like a duck.

Today was not the day I expected him to ask.

"You think he put this together all by himself?" Mia asks, pulling away and holding me by the shoulders. Vibrant red tendrils frame her face as a sinister smile begins to spread.

"Y-You kn-knew?" I stutter, looking over her shoulder to where Spencer and Jay are embracing in a man-hug.

"We all knew. I can't believe you didn't suspect anything. Hell, if Spencer had relented, there would've been a double wedding today."

My mouth is slightly ajar as Jay and Spencer join us, Spence wrapping his arms around Mia's waist and pulling his bride against his chest. Jay mimics his actions, his warm embrace calming my racing heart.

Until he leans down and nibbles the lobe of my ear before kissing the sweet spot on the side of my neck. Pregnancy has my hormones running wild, especially the last few weeks. All it takes it the simplest touch, a devious look, and I'm jumping Jay's bones. It doesn't matter where we are or who's around.

Once my engine is revved, I can't wait.

And he knows how to get it purring.

"I love you," Jay says, his lips teasing my neck.

"I love you, too."

My body is humming with anticipation the rest of the reception. The urge to leave, to run, is overwhelming. Last year running would have meant away from my friends. Away from Jay, from the feelings I was trying to fight. Now, it means running toward him. This very moment? It means running with him. To the home we share. Where our bed lays unmade thanks to our pre-wedding activities.

"Ready?" Jay finally asks as Mia and Spencer make their exit.

They're off to spend two weeks in paradise. Sunshine, fruity drinks, and white, sandy beaches.

"I've been ready. The question is," I start as I place my hand in his, giving it a little tug, "can you handle me?"

"You were put on this Earth for me and only me. I was made to handle whatever you throw at me."

"Even if it's a swollen belly?" I joke as we push through the doors of Riley's, the chill of the spring night wrapping itself around me, cooling my body instantly.

Pulling me to a stop and pressing me against the passenger door of our car, Jay leans in close and whispers in my ear, "You're the most beautiful pregnant woman I've ever seen. Knowing there's a mini version of you growing in there makes you even more beautiful. I'd keep you pregnant the rest of our life together if I thought you'd let me."

Laughing, I place my hands on his chest and push but he doesn't budge.

"One kid at a time. Not to mention I have a feeling our son is going to be just like his daddy. At least I hope so."

"Oh yeah. You want another me in this world?" Jay's hands travel from my hips, lower and lower until they reach the hem of my skirt, slipping beneath and slowly traveling back upward, toward where I want them the most. Toward the ache I've been trying to ignore the last two hours since he proposed in front of the entire town.

"I take it back," I say, suddenly breathless as his hands continue their slow climb. "One of you is plenty."

Jay's hands disappear, the passenger door is opening, and I'm being helped in the car before I can register what's happening.

"What the hell?" I practically scream at him as he takes his place behind the wheel.

"Home." His words are a demand, not a request. "I'm not having sex with my fiancée for the first time in a parking lot."

There's a smile on my face the entire ten-minute drive to the house we share on the outskirts of town knowing the effect I have on him. My smile disappears as we pull into our driveway, hitting the first bump in the dirt, warm liquid soaking my underwear.

"Jay." The concern in my voice causes him to slam the brakes, my body jolting forward. Jay's arm shoots across my chest, stopping me from slamming into the dashboard.

"What's wrong?" His words are rushed as he looks me up and down.

"It's time."

"Time?" he asks, wrinkling his brow. The moment my words sink in, his eyes go wide. "Now?"

All I can do is nod my head as Jay throws the car in reverse, backing over the same bump as the first stabbing pain hits low in my back, sending searing pain through my lower region.

———

It turns out Sammy does take after me. He was a stubborn child from the moment my water broke. After close to thirty-nine hours of labor, he finally made his appearance. On the sixth anniversary of Sam's murder. Two and a half weeks ahead of schedule.

He was perfectly healthy with ten tiny fingers and toes. A head full of dark brown hair that swooped to the side and bright blue eyes. When he smiles, he has a tiny dimple in his left cheek, just like his daddy.

"How is my handsome nephew today?" Spence asks as he walks through the nursery door.

Spencer and Mia cut their honeymoon short when they heard Sammy was born. We waited to call them until after he arrived, knowing they would want to jump on a plane and come back. Mia's wrath at finding out two days after he was born was scary, but the second Sammy was cradled in her arms the anger melted away.

One shared look with Spencer and I knew what was coming next for them. It took all of two months for her to announce they were pregnant.

"He's being a grouch and not wanting to take a nap."

Scooping him out of my arms, Spencer blows raspberries on Sammy's naked belly, causing both of them to giggle.

"I'll get him to sleep. Why don't you visit with Mia for a bit?" His words have a warning tone in them. Mia's been a temperamental mama since the start of her second trimester. Her moods are as fiery as her hair most days.

"Good luck," I say, pushing out of the rocking chair and moving toward the door. I swear I hear Spencer whisper, "You too," but when I turn around, his eyes are closed and he's slowly rocking as he holds Sammy against his chest.

Spencer is going to make an amazing dad. He's so calming and gentle with Sammy. He can get him to sleep in a matter of minutes when it takes me an hour. I'm happy for the reprieve but also scared of what is waiting for me in my kitchen. I'm praying today is one of Mia's good days.

"Hey," I greet her as I cross the threshold, kissing Jay on the cheek before moving to hug my best friend. "How are you feeling today?"

"Fine I guess. She was kicking me in the bladder earlier and I pissed myself but otherwise it's been a good day. I think the morning sickness is finally over." Mia's morning sickness lasted all day. Hearing that it's over is the best news I've had in weeks.

"That's great. I'm glad you're feeling better."

Taking the seat next to her at the table, she shows me the most recent ultrasound picture. We talk about the nursery and her upcoming baby shower. It's not long before Spencer and Jay join us at the table, a grim expression on Spencer's face. Mia sits back, concern consuming her features. When I look to Jay for answers, his lips are pressed together, as if he doesn't approve of what's about to happen.

"What?" I ask, not really wanting to know the answer, the single word slipping out before I can stop myself.

"The chief released the evidence from Sam's case since Ben was sentenced last week."

"Okayyy," I say, dragging out the y in confusion. "Why

does everyone look like they're upset with this fact? That's great. We've been waiting a year and a half for him to be sentenced. I'm glad it's finally over, aren't you?"

Looking around the table, the three of them nod in agreement as Spencer slides an envelope across the table toward me. My name is scribbled across the front in handwriting I would recognize anywhere.

She always dotted her I's with a heart.

"What's this?" I ask, staring at the envelope but not reaching for it.

"It was in Sam's apron," Spencer explains.

My next breath is audible as I suck it deep in my lungs, holding it for a few beats before slowly releasing it.

"What's in it?" I ask, looking at Spencer, but it's Jay who answers my question.

"It's your graduation card."

Turning to face my fiancé, I try to decipher the pained expression on his face. He knew about this, kept it from me, more than likely because he didn't have a choice. Is he concerned I'd be mad at him for that or the fact that he just admitted to opening the card?

"You should read it, Andi," Spencer urges. "When you're ready."

Without another word, Spencer and Mia leave. My eyes are glued to the envelope in front of me, to the heart above the I in my name.

Sam.

Even after all this time, thinking about her brings tears to my eyes and a pain in my heart. Where I once held guilt for my part in her death, in betraying her, there is now only sorrow for what happened to my friend. For the life that was stolen for her.

Acceptance healed most of my wounds but not all of

them, which is why I now help others manage their grief. We all grieve differently. There are no magic words to help you heal, to manage the pain, to fix a broken heart.

They say time heals all wounds.

I say time dulls the pain.

Until moments like these where something like an envelope with a little heart on it will bring fresh tears to your eyes and grief rears its ugly head.

Good friends. Family. They all help you heal. Their support is invaluable.

If it weren't for Jay, Spencer, and Mia, I wouldn't be where I am today. But most of all, I have Summer to thank. Without her love and forgiveness, none of us would have been able to look at ourselves in the mirror. She really helped us see what happened for what it was.

Fate.

Because according to Sam, everything happens for a reason. That encompasses all things in life. From me silently loving Jay all those years to Ben Royal losing his shit and killing her that night.

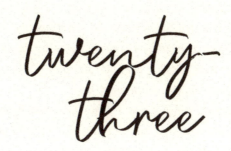

twenty-three

"I'm right here if you want me to open it with you," Jay offers, sliding into the seat next to me.

"Why was this in her apron? Graduation was a month away."

"There was one in there for me, too." My head whips in his direction at his confession. "Which is why I think you should open yours. If it says what I think it says, you'll feel better after reading what she wrote. I promise."

After a few deep breaths, I reach for the envelope, turning it over in my hands a few times before lifting the flap. Jay's chair scrapes against the floor as he pushes away from the table. I place my hand on his leg as he stands, and when he looks down at me and our eyes meet, he reads the message my heart is sending him.

Sitting back down, he scoots his chair closer, wraps his arm around my shoulders, and pulls me close. Leaning my head against his chest, I pull the card from the confines of the once bright yellow envelope. It's a standard congratulations card for a college graduate. A mortarboard and tassel are on the front, the word 'Congratulations' in colorful letters across the top of the card.

As I open it, my eyes forgo the card's print and instead focus on Sam's handwriting.

Andi,

You are the greatest friend a girl could ask for and I'm proud to call you my bestie. I know you're leaving me and starting the next chapter of your life, but I think there's something I need to confess before you go.

I'm a horribly selfish friend. I should have been honest with you the second I realized the truth. Instead, I let the sting of pain consume me. If I was miserable, everyone needed to be. But that ends now. None of this is your fault, or Jay's. It's mine. For holding on to him when it was obvious I needed to let him go. For keeping you two apart when we all know you were meant to be together.

I love you both and all I want is for you to be happy.

If you love him, the way I think you do, the way I know he loves you, know that the next move is yours. Be together. Be happy. Start the next chapter of your life with him. Don't run away from how you feel the way you've been doing all these years. You deserve this.

One day I can only hope to find the kind of love that I see you two have for one another.

Your best friend, forever and always, no matter what ...

Sam

Tears are freely streaming down my face as I close the card, pulling it to my chest and hugging it tight.

"She knew," I whisper.

"I know." Jay runs his hand up and down my back as the tears continue to fall.

"She never said a word. She could have thrown it in our faces. Called us out, but she didn't. Why? Why did she stand back and watch in silence? Why didn't she confront us?"

"I have no idea, but if I had to guess, she was probably trying to figure that out for herself."

"How long do you think?"

"How long what?" he asks as I sit up so I can assess his reaction.

"When did she figure it out? Weeks before this? Months? Years?"

My mind frantically tries to recall any indication of Sam knowing. Of her questioning the situation. All I can think about is the summer before senior year. All the trips she planned and tried to back out of, urging us to go without her.

"My best guess would be she was suspicious from the start, but New Year's Eve could have been when she confirmed her suspicions. After you left, I couldn't go to bed. I was wired, I wanted to chase after you. Kiss you again. Make you see that we were meant for each other. When I finally went upstairs, Sam was wide awake. She was just sitting there, knees pulled to her chest, crying. When I asked her what was wrong, she just shook her head and cried harder.

"If she saw us kiss, she never said anything. After that, we both pulled away from her, from each other. Then she was gone. Life is a bit blurry after that, but the one thing I do remember is the expression on her face the night before I left for vacation. It always felt like she was saying good-bye to me. I brushed it off as a figment of my imagination because she died, but the more I think about it, the more it makes sense. She wrote these while we were gone."

"What did yours say?" I ask, sliding my card back into the envelope and flipping it over so I can stare at the little heart again.

"The same thing yours did basically. That she loved me but wanted me to be happy. She knew I was in love with you and made me promise to be good to you, to take care of you, to love you the way you deserve to be loved."

Memories of the morning I left for spring break flash through my mind. The look of devastation on Sam's face. I always assumed she was sad because she was going to be alone for the week. Now I can see the hurt in her eyes. The pain in her stare. The concern in her voice as it shook while pleading with me.

She wanted time alone with me before she dropped her knowledge bomb. Time without Jay around. Time where it was just the two of us. Best friends hanging out.

Hoes before bros.

What she'll never know is that I'd always choose her over a guy. She was my sister at heart. If she didn't want me to be with Jay, if she asked me to stay away from him, I would've. My heart may have shattered in my chest, but I wouldn't have given it a second thought.

"What now?" I ask. "I don't know where to go from here."

"What do you mean?"

"Sam gave us her blessing. We didn't deserve it then and we don't now. I don't know what to make of this," I say, motioning to the envelope on the table.

"I think we take her words to heart. We spend the rest of our life proving that there was a reason we couldn't stay away from each other back then, that we were meant to be together, to love each other with our whole hearts. We get married this summer the way we're planning to. We have nine more kids and live happily ever after."

"Nine!" I screech, slapping my hand over my mouth and closing my eyes, hoping my voice didn't carry up the stairs to where Sammy is sleeping thanks to Uncle Spencer.

"Fine, seven, but you're not getting me to go any lower," Jay jokes, wiggling his eyebrows at me.

"You'll be lucky to get two more out of me, Mr. Ross."

"Ooh. So formal. And what if I want three more, Mrs. Soon-to-be Ross?"

"One step at a time. You put a ring on it. It would be nice to be Mrs. Ross before popping out another mini you." Leaning in close, I press my lips against his as I say, "But that doesn't mean we can't practice."

"Are you sure you're not pregnant already? You're awfully horny these days," he notes before pulling me close and capturing my lips with his.

When I finally pull away, breathless, I mentally calculate the last time I had my period, rule out pregnancy, then drag my soon-to-be-husband up to our room to practice. We barely get across the threshold when Sammy wakes up, his screams echoing down the hall as I reach for the button of Jay's jeans.

"I'll get him," Jay offers, kissing me on the forehead before leaving me and my raging hormones standing in the middle of the room.

And he wants nine more?

I laugh at the thought of ten kids running around the yard as Jay and I watch from the swing he hung from the front porch last weekend. Ten might be a bit too many for me but I'm not opposed to having more. Especially when I see my sexy-ass-fiancé walk back in the room, shirtless, with our son pressed to his chest.

"Someone was missing his mama I think," he says as Sammy catches sight of me, wiggling his entire body, a huge grin on his face.

All I can do is smile. I couldn't be happier with the way my life is turning out. I only wish Sam was here to be a part of it. Though, there are times I swear she is here, watching over all of us. Keeping us safe. Smiling down.

"There's something I think I'd like to do," I say to Jay as I situate myself on our bed, resting against the headboard with Sammy curled in my arms. "I've been thinking about it all week, but I want your opinion."

"Okayyy," he says, drawing out the word. Nervous curiosity looks adorable on him.

"I want to talk to Ben Royal."

"Why?" he asks before I can continue.

Shooting him a look that screams 'calm down' he nods his head and takes a seat at the end of the bed facing me.

"I want to interview him. I want to complete the profile. I *need* to complete it."

"What's nagging at you?" he inquires, knowing I'm leaving out the most important facts.

"It was too easy. He was a textbook case, yet he went undiscovered for five years. Yes, the police screwed up, overlooked things, but I think there's more to the story than we know. I want a complete profile, one without holes in it, and I want to write a book. The story of Sam's murder."

"A book? Like a murder mystery?" Jay wrinkles his brow in confusion.

"No. I want to write her story. I want the world to know what an amazing person she was. It'll be more of a biography of her life, told through the eyes of the people who knew her best. And part of it will be told through Ben's eyes."

Letting my confession sink in, Jay stares at me for a few minutes before finally nodding his head.

"What can I do to help?"

"I need to talk to him," I state firmly, my voice strong even though the words cause my heart to stop in my chest at the thought of confronting him.

———

"I'M RECORDING THIS CONVERSATION FOR RESEARCH purposes. Anything you say cannot be used against you in a court of law. Do you understand?" I ask, staring into his dark brown eyes. They're filled with humor; the way most killers' eyes are.

They find it amusing that I want to speak with them. It feeds their ego. They get to relive their crimes and enjoy the high all over again all by telling me their story.

This man is no different than any other murderer.

He may have killed my best friend but that doesn't make him special.

Yes, I've taken a special interest in him, but that's personal.

"I understand. Just like I did last week when we talked. And the week before that."

"Thank you. Now, Mr. Royal—"

"Ben. Please call me Ben. Mr. Royal was my father, and he was not a good man."

And you are? I want to ask.

"Okay, Ben. We've talked about how you met Sam in high school. The jealousy you felt when she dated your brother, Brandon. And reconnecting with her when you moved back to town. You've explained what you loved about Sam and how you wanted to be with her. You even described in detail the events leading up to the night you killed her."

"It was an accident," he insists, for the millionth time.

You don't accidentally carry a tire iron around in a backpack and you certainly don't accidentally hit someone over the head with it. It's called premeditated murder, but I don't correct him. That isn't why I'm here.

"Yes, the night of the accident. Can you tell me what happened that night?"

I've been interviewing Ben Royal once a week for the last month. We're getting to the hardest part of the interview. The night he killed her. I'm not ready for it, I know this, but I also know the story won't be complete without all the facts. So, I had him start at the beginning.

Meeting Sam. Falling in love with her. Showering her with gifts in high school, when she was only in ninth grade. He wanted her even back then. Wanted to make her his. He also admitted to being aware that she would never want to date him because he was a screw up.

Ben was a star athlete but a poor student. The only reason he passed was because his brother, Brandon, who was a freshman at the time, helped him with his homework. Ben was the brawn and Brandon the brains of the family. Ben had failed kindergarten twice, making him a nineteen-year-old senior.

The verbal abuse from his father started at an early age and never let up.

The only reason he came back home was to watch his father die a painful death from lung cancer. When his mother asked him to take over the theater, he agreed so he could be close to her. Then he ran into Sam again. She was older this time, a sophomore in college. And he found her even more infatuating.

Sam had recently started dating Jay and it enraged Ben. In his mind, Jay wasn't good enough for her. No one was but him. She belonged to Ben, and he wasn't going to let anyone stand in his way.

So, he watched and waited for the perfect moment to strike.

We had it all wrong, though. His sights weren't set on Sam. He wanted Jay. He wanted him out of the way so they could be together. In his mind, Jay was the problem and if he removed him from the equation, Sam would seek comfort from Ben. The way she had the night at the theater when she was upset.

He bought the rope and tape from a neighboring town. Stored them in his backpack along with the tire iron and carried it everywhere with him. He was on his way to Riley's that night, assuming Jay would be waiting in the parking lot to pick Sam up after work the way he always did. When he saw her walking home, alone, he approached her.

Offered to walk with her.

She turned him down.

He persisted, attempting to take her hand, and she pushed him away.

Sam was a spitfire. If she wasn't interested in you or you were getting too pushy, she wasn't afraid to tell you. Her lack of a filter that night was what sent Ben into a fit of rage. He tried to calm her down, to control her, but Sam struggled to get away from him. When he thought he heard someone coming he took the tire iron out of his bag and struck her over the head, planning to knock her out, and carried her to the small, hidden enclosure of the park. The couple entered the park as he was tying her up. He panicked. He hadn't intended on hurting Sam. Jay was his target.

He screwed up and he knew it. Knowing he'd need an

alibi in case anyone stumbled on Sam, he went to Riley's, had one drink per usual, and walked back through the park to see if the couple was still there. He watched them run out, rain falling in sheets, drenching everyone and everything.

When he went back to where he left Sam, she wasn't breathing. He hadn't intended to kill her. He only wanted to subdue her so he could talk to her. To explain how they were meant to be together.

He goes into detail about how he covered his tracks. About how he felt knowing she was dead. That he had killed the one woman he loved.

Not a single tear is shed by either of us as he speaks. When I finally turn the recorder off and leave the room, I fall to a heap on the floor and let myself cry.

For my friend. For myself. For everyone who knew Sam.

"That's it, right? You're done now?" Jay asks, as I slide into the passenger seat.

"I'm done. I have everything I need to complete the book and he's going to rot in hell for what he did to Sam, whether he intended to kill her or not."

I don't plan to tell Jay he was Ben's original target. There's no need. It won't change the facts of the case. It won't be included in Sam's biography, but the profile I'll be writing will have all the facts.

Telling him the truth will only hurt him. There's no reason for him to feel any blame for her death, and I know that's where his mind will go. It's not his fault. The only person to blame here is Ben Royal.

"Where to?" he asks, taking my hand in his after shifting the car into drive.

"Home. I want to go home."

Wherever I am, as long as Jay's by my side, feels like home.

THE END!

Made in USA - North Chelmsford, MA
1313333_9798505934302
05.05.2022 0809